IN THE MIDDLE

S. J. Henderson

A Tiny Fox Press Book

Library of Congress Catalog Card Number: 2016921247

ISBN: 978-1-946501-04-2

Tiny Fox Press and the book fox logo are all registered trademarks of Tiny Fox Press LLC

Tiny Fox Press LLC
North Port, FL

Also by S. J. Henderson

Middle Grade

Daniel the Draw-er

"This pencil is no ordinary pencil," says the cat sitting on the end of nine-year-old Daniel's bed. "It's magic."

Everything Daniel draws with his enchanted pencil comes to life, from a talking cat named Whiskers to a group of pizza-loving aliens from the planet Beezo. Daniel's mom said she wanted him to make new friends. This probably isn't what she meant.

Join Daniel and his fantastic creatures on this fun-for-the-whole-family adventure as he discovers that friendship is the greatest magic of all . . . and that it can be found in the most unusual of places.

Daniel the Camp-er

There are a few simple rules Daniel follows:

Rule One: never let an adult see your weakness. Daniel made that mistake and look where he ended up—summer camp.

Rule Two: never make fun of the person who feeds you, unless you like Miss Gunderson's peppery pancakes and green hamburgers.

Rule Three: stay away from girls who love Glitter Ponies. They have cooties, after all.

And Rule Four: never, ever lose your magic pencil.

But Daniel has broken all of his own rules. Now he's stuck and starving at Camp Bigfoot with the school bully as his bunkmate and an ooey-gooey girl who won't leave him alone. If all of that wasn't bad enough, his prized possession, a pencil that brings his drawings to life, has gone missing and wacky creatures are popping up all over camp.

Can Daniel survive Camp Bigfoot and find his magic pencil before it's too late?

Anthologies

Skywriters Ring Anthology: Short Story Collection

Includes S. J. Henderson's Young Adult Fantasy story, "For Eve."

Mosaic: a Compilation of Creative Writing

Includes S. J. Henderson's short stories "Bees," and "Daniel the Draw-er Makes a Friend."

For two little lovebirds who flew away home.

Walking with you was never a burden.

Chapter 1

Eighteen days ago I took my first step.

A nurse with a bouncy blonde ponytail and a chirpy voice thought it would be a stellar idea to buy me a cake to celebrate. It had vanilla frosting, and loopy red letters scrawled across the top wished me a "Happy Birthday!"

When I pointed out my birthday wasn't for, like, five more months, her dimpled cheeks turned pink. She mumbled something about "new beginnings," and Nurse Greta shushed her before she could say anything else wrong. Good thing, too, because I would've punched her in her annoyingly perky face if I hadn't been exhausted from taking my one step.

New beginnings, my butt.

And now here I am. Stuck in a taxi, the absolute last place I'd rather be, traveling to my aunt's house, where I'll begin my new life. Whatever that means.

The taxi's tire thuds into a pothole, and I clutch the seat until my knuckles turn white. Within my chest my heart gallops wildly, and I take a deep breath to calm myself. Of all the things that could go wrong in an automobile, a heart attack seems the most ironic. I mean, you're driving along, all happy and safe one minute, then your body just up and quits on you. Then it's *crash—adios!*

Yeah, cars aren't really my thing.

I lean forward towards the driver, a middle-aged guy wearing a faded baseball cap and a grey t-shirt that's definitely seen better days. The photo ID affixed to the back of his seat informs me his name is Bud. He looks like a Bud.

"How much longer?" I raise my voice above the annoying twang of the song he hums along with. Talking hurts my brain, and I press my palm to my forehead to slow the vibration. Everyone thinks I keep quiet because I want my space. And, yes, I want people to leave me alone—but most of all I want this God-awful pain to disappear. Keeping my mouth shut helps, or, at least, makes me less interesting. If I'm boring, no one expects me to perform like a circus animal.

"We should be to Mitte in, oh, 'bout five minutes. You okay, Miss?" The driver's red-rimmed eyes peek at me from the rearview mirror.

I nod in response, but he's already turned his focus back to the road. A stab of discomfort zings up my neck from the motion, and I suck in a hissing breath. Bud doesn't seem to notice, but I don't mind. I've reached the limit of how many times I can lie about feeling good.

I hope my aunt won't take it upon herself to solve all of my problems once I step foot inside her house. Everyone thinks they can make me all better, but no one's succeeded. If she tries fixing me, I'll probably self-combust.

Before the accident, Aunt Perdita showed zero interest in me, existing only in old photo albums. She began as a pink, wide-eyed baby with a bow someone must have taped to her bare scalp; she morphed into a tan, lean young woman framed by a mane of golden hair. And then the pictures stopped, as if she'd simply disappeared. Mom never talked about my aunt, and the mere mention of her name brought tears to Mom's eyes. I'd always assumed she'd died in some tragic way and Mom didn't want to relive it, so I never pressed for more information. Obviously, I'd assumed wrong, since each passing second brings me closer to my only remaining relative.

Mitte, my new town, is a mystery to me, too. Nancy, the social worker at the hospital, couldn't find it on a map, even after poking around on the internet. She acted nervous about sending me somewhere without concrete proof the place even existed. Aunt Perdita proved to be influential, handling all the details of getting me from my hospital room in Detroit to her house in Mitte. Bud at least acts like he knows the direction of this secret destination, so I have to trust him. I don't usually make it a practice of trusting pot-bellied dudes who listen to whiny music for fun, but I am running low on options.

The driver tips his head to the right. "Here we are."

Where "here" is, I'm not exactly sure. The lonesome two-lane road stretches on ahead, embraced on either side by an endless evergreen forest. Moving from the city is bound to mean a lot of changes, but this is kind of ridiculous. I can't even see my new town.

A large piece of stone—some kind of sign, maybe—stands a lonely guard just off the shoulder of the road, the only indication that the taxi hasn't slipped into some kind of labyrinth. Carvings lace across its weather-worn top. As we pass by, I twist around in my seat for a better look, but our speed blurs the words or pictures or maybe just the careless meanderings of an insect. Just before the hunk of rock fades from view, a dark figure shifts from the cover of the trees. A person.

Maybe that's what the people do for fun in the boonies: carve stuff on old statues. I imagine some lonely tattoo artist sulking in the forest, forced to practice his art on whatever he can find because the good citizens of Mitte don't want their skin defiled. I smile at the idea because it's completely dumb.

The town springs up like turning the page in a pop-up book. Granted, there's not much to see. Little shops and offices surround the main street. Beyond that, mounds of flowers curl up at the feet of a sputtering fountain. Several rows of weathered limestone benches angle around the water. Staring at fountains and carving trees, Mitte's main attractions. Riveting.

The town is dead. At home, people stroll with their dogs down the sidewalks, chit-chat with each other outside of the restaurants, drive their cars to work, pedal bikes to wherever people pedal bikes. Totally not the case here in Mitte. Besides Bud and me, no one else ventures out into public. Each manicured lawn sits empty, and no faces peer out from the windows of the postage-stamp houses we pass. I pray this isn't one of those crazy towns so fearful of outsiders that everyone hides deep within their shelters until the scary thing—me— passes.

Aunt Perdita has yet to speak a single word to me, ever, but somehow she'd convinced the social worker that Mitte would be the perfect place for me to heal. Eyeing row after row of lifeless homes and empty streets, I'm not sure I agree with her.

Before long, Bud pulls up to a wrought iron gate. Before he can even roll down his window to push the call button on the security keypad, the gate swings inward, granting us access. Someone's expecting me.

Bud follows the long, shrub-lined drive to the footsteps of the largest building I've seen so far. The house gleams white, with tall pillars in front that look like they came straight from a cotton plantation. My stomach knots with anxiety. The only place I'd ever called home had three bedrooms and a tiny speck of a yard. If this is my new casa, I'm in way over my head.

Bud climbs out of the car and opens my door for me. "This is it, Miss."

My mouth hangs open as I step out of the taxi. I can't believe Aunt Perdita lives here, in the kind of house I'd only seen in the movies. Maybe this was the reason she and my parents hadn't kept in touch. My folks weren't greedy or jealous people, but money can make people do things they normally wouldn't.

I wait for Bud to retrieve my suitcase from the trunk, then turn to him. "What do I owe you? I'm sure my aunt—"

He blinks a few times, clears his throat, then waves me off with his baseball-mitt-sized paw. "Nah. It's the least I can do."

Someone must have told him my story.

"Well, thank you," I murmur, looking at my feet. I don't want to be the poor orphan girl everyone pities.

When I turn back to him to offer a late smile for his thoughtfulness, he isn't there. And neither is the taxi. The doctors told me I might lose track of time every now and then because of my head injuries, but this is the first time I've spaced out long enough for an entire guy and his vehicle to disappear. Life's officially strange.

A man with skin the color of coffee stands up from where he'd been working on the other side of the hedgerow. I add him to one more detail I'd blanked out on, and paste on a thin smile. All I want to do is get inside the house, find a room, and be by myself. I don't want to meet anyone, not even my long-lost aunt. And certainly not the guy running toward me with shears in hand.

No running with sharp objects, mister. Doesn't everyone know that?

He closes in on me quick. "How'd you do it?"

"W-what?" I glance around. Mitte's official welcoming committee needs a little guidance on being more, well, *welcoming.*

"How'd you do it?" The man is upon me now, grasping me by the shoulders. The blades of the shears dance inches from my earlobe, but I'm in too much pain to worry about him lopping off the side of my face. Fire erupts in my body, traveling from the top of my head down to the middle of the back as he jostles me. If he keeps it up, I'll be begging for the shears soon.

"Norman, leave her be," a man's voice calls from the side of the house.

Norman's eyes bulge in desperation as he looks toward whoever had spoken. "But she knows somethin', Oliver. Bud, he just—"

Another guy, young and tan like someone who hasn't spent the last umpteenth months basking in the ultraviolet glow of the hospital, saunters around the corner and into view. His slow movement worries me, especially since Norman still holds me in his white-knuckled grip. This Oliver, whoever he is, hasn't completely convinced my new friend to let go. I force myself to focus on Oliver as he approaches, trying to keep myself from crying at the searing pain in my spine.

Oliver comes up next to us, careful to choose the side farthest from the hedge trimmers, and lays a hand on Norman's shoulder. "Norm. She doesn't know."

Norman pinches his eyelids closed and drops his head. Slowly, he slides his hands from my shoulders and down to his side. I wrap my arms around myself and draw in a shaky breath.

"Sorry, ma'am. Norman here mistook you for someone else," Oliver says, tipping his head. His slick, dark hair falls across one of his eyes, and he swipes it away with the back of his hand.

"No harm done," I lie, gritting my teeth as the pain recedes.

"I'm Oliver." He offers me his hand and I leave him hanging while I decide whether or not he's insane.

"Lucy," I say finally, placing my hand in his.

He smiles, and his eyes squint so they're nearly non-existent. If I even cared about guys anymore, I would totally find Oliver adorable. With my whole world in ruins, adorable guys and romance don't really register on my radar. It hurts to be alive. I can't possibly ask another human being to share in my misery.

"I like that name."

I nod and look away. Small talk isn't my forte.

Oliver, who must have sensed my lack of interest, clears his throat. "You're Perdita's niece?"

"I guess."

A grin spreads across his face. "You guess? What kind of answer is that? Are you or aren't you?"

"Look," I say, glancing toward the mansion's front door. "I don't know her from you or Norman, but I honestly don't think it's any of your business. Now, if you'll excuse me."

Oliver puts his hands in front of his chest, palm-out, in surrender. "My apologies, ma'am. I only meant to be friendly, I swear."

"Sorry, I'm not looking for friendship." With a streak of stubbornness, I pick up my suitcase. The jolt of pain makes me sick to my stomach.

It takes great effort to move forward with my limp, another souvenir from the accident. The doctors tried to give me hope by telling me most of my physical complaints will fade over time. Except the limp. The force of impact snapped my femur in three places, and they'd pinned and glued me together the best they could. Unfortunately, their best wasn't enough to secure my spot back on the track team. I'll never run again, at least not unless I'm being chased. Hindered by the weight of my lonely suitcase, even walking up the stone steps to the front door seems impossible.

"Let me help." Oliver places his hand on mine. "Please."

I stick out my chin and square my shoulders, desperate to demonstrate what little strength I have left. His brown eyes meet mine unexpectedly, and my resolve melts away.

"Sooner or later you'll return the favor, Lucy." He smiles just enough to crease his cheek with a dimple.

A *dimple*. Before Oliver, I'd never seen a grown man with dimples. Before the accident, Oliver's charm would've made me giddy. Now that I've been reconstructed and reanimated like Dr. Frankenstein's monster, I feel nothing at all.

Chapter 2

Like every horror movie I'd ever seen, the heavy white door creaks open as I reach for the doorknocker.

"Hello?" I peek inside the house. My words echo in the entryway and inside my skull. "Anyone home?"

No one answers. I hesitate for a moment before taking a step inside. Oliver waits on the porch, my suitcase in hand, until I look back at him with a forced smile.

"Just leave it right there, thanks," I instruct in a small voice, but even a whisper reverberates in this big, open space. The fear in my voice shocks me.

Oliver meets my gaze without blinking. "With all due respect, ma'am, I've been raised to carry heavy burdens for those who can't."

"Okay, you've *got* to stop calling me 'ma'am.' I'm younger than you by a few years, I bet. Totally not a 'ma'am'."

"I meant nothing by it, just being courteous," he replies, following a few steps behind me as I limp further into the foyer.

If courtesy rates so high on his list of priorities, I wish he would push ahead of me and venture into the house first. I've seen this movie before. Spoiler alert: the virgin chick always dies first, an ax buried smack dab between her eyes. With all the heavy metal in my brain now, the ax would probably break before my head does. Somehow, I don't find much comfort in that.

My companion seems to pick up on the rattling in my knees and speeds in front of me with his chest puffed up proudly. I pretend to be annoyed by his bravado, but I exhale as soon as he's not looking.

"Miss Perdita," Oliver calls, striding over to a doorway on our right.

She appears through the door straight ahead of us, sliding her reading glasses from her nose and pushing them up on top of her golden head. "Honestly, Oliver. What's the meaning of all this racket?"

The roundest part of his cheeks pink. He avoids her glare. "I'm sorry to raise my voice, Miss Perdita. Your niece—"

My aunt squints her crystal eyes to see past him to where I stand. "Lucille? Is that you?"

I shudder. No one calls me Lucille and lives. No one. "Yeah, it's me. But, please, call me Lucy."

I've replayed this moment, our very first meeting, a hundred times over the past couple of days. Aunt Perdita would greet me at the doorway, smelling like fresh chocolate chip cookies and rose water. We wouldn't need pathetic introductions, because we would be too busy weeping for the loss of her sister and my mother. The major flaw in that scenario becomes glaringly obvious as I notice the hard lines etching her features. We are strangers.

Instead of an embrace, she offers me a watered-down smile. At least I think it's a smile. Maybe it's indigestion. I used to make that same face after eating a big bowl of Mom's chili. She always made it too spicy. Remembering the last chili night with Mom and Dad makes my heart twist within my chest, and I take a deep breath. If I hope to survive without my parents, I need to stop thinking about them. I suppose my therapist at the hospital would disagree, telling me to embrace all of the good times we shared. Really, though, I don't know what the therapist would say because I never went to see her.

After several seconds of uncomfortable silence, Aunt Perdita finally clears her throat. "Well, then. Oliver, help Lucil—*Lucy* to her room, won't you?"

Oliver nods and turns to me. "C'mon, it's this way."

I trudge after him, the *thu-thump* of my uneven gait deafening on the marble floors. Each step makes me more and more self-conscious, until I finally can't stand it anymore. "Are you my uncle?" I blurt.

He stops in his tracks and looks over his shoulder at me. There's that dimple again. My cheeks flush, embarrassed by my lack of social grace more than anything else.

"No," he says simply.

"Then how do you know so much about my aunt's house?"

"Oh, well . . . You know what they say about small towns."

My eyebrows scrunch up and I shake my head. "Nope, I don't know what *they say*. I'm a city girl."

He resumes his slow processional down the hall. "Everyone knows everything about everybody else, that's what they say. Mitte's no exception."

I don't care what Oliver says; it's still weird that he knows his way around the house.

The corridor stretches on a long way. I'm not used to walking long distances, so my gimpy leg protests with each step. Finally, he stops at an open doorway on the right side of the hall. "Here it is," he announces, "home sweet home."

I know he's just trying to make me feel more comfortable, but I want to lash out at him. This isn't home, and it never will be. Instead of my canopy bed draped with sheer scarves the shade of ripened plums, there is a queen-sized bed covered in a grey down comforter. The walls are painted white, the hint of sunlight filtering through the thin curtains setting them aglow. The brightness is too much and I squint against it. Hopefully someone remembered to pack my sunglasses because I'll need them to step foot inside my own bedroom. Great.

After turning a full circle to take in my new space, I'm surprised to see Oliver still standing next to my suitcase. I'd hoped he would read my mind and leave me alone.

"Uh, thanks," I mutter.

He doesn't move. I wonder if maybe something is wrong with Oliver.

"I'm going to take a nap now, so if you don't mind . . ."

Oliver stands there for another second or two before he blinks out of his daze. "Oh. *Oh!* Right. I'm sorry. You're probably really tired."

"Yeah." I barely nod, trying to keep the pain from shooting through me again. "Long trip."

"It was nice to meet you, then. I'll be seeing you, Lucy." He winks, then turns on his heel and leaves.

Part of me wants to chase him down and punch him in the eye so he can't wink at me ever again—the nerve! And part of me wants to beg him to stay. My new room feels too empty without him here, which is completely ridiculous. We just met.

Instead of unpacking what's left of my worldly possessions, I collapse onto the bed and stare at the ceiling until sleep finds me. Sleep remains the only thing I can manage without pain, and even that's debatable. Sometimes when I sleep I forget about everything: the argument. The God-awful shriek of metal. The blare of the horn. The crying. When I'm awake, I can't escape the nightmares.

I'm not sure how long I stay asleep because there's no clock in this joint. Besides, my watch had been discarded along the way, another thing lost to the crash. Even if it had survived, I would've stopped wearing it anyway. IVs and my wristwatch sound like a pretty horrible combo.

The light filtering through my thin curtains might be fading, or it could be the start of a migraine. If I cared enough, I could hobble over to the window to check where the sun hangs in the sky to get a better idea. But I don't, so I don't.

I lay there for a while until my stomach starts to protest. The more I try to ignore it, the louder it groans and grumbles. I glance at the bedroom door, not looking forward to snooping around the mansion in search of food. When my stomach gurgles again, I sigh and kick my legs over the side of the bed.

The hallway stretches on endlessly without Oliver to keep me company. I curse Aunt Perdita for banishing me to the furthest end of the house, or so it seems, as I pass dozens of white doors on either side of me—probably all bedrooms. Certainly someone must have warned her about my condition. This is probably her way of sneaking in physical therapy or something. Whatever her reasoning, it doesn't matter. I'm determined to be mad at her anyway.

Out of breath and trembling, I finally reach the foyer. Another long corridor identical to the one I'd just traveled lies ahead. To my left there's a closed door, the one Aunt Perdita had come through when we met earlier. I decide to continue straight, which leads me down the hallway lined with more white doors. Luckily the first door on my left is propped open, and from the doorway I spy a long marble counter. The enticing aroma of something—*anything*—cooking drifts into the hall. With my mouth watering, I clomp inside.

"Oh dear," squeaks an old woman bent over a boiling pot on the stove. "You gave me a fright."

I blush and drop my gaze to the tile floor. "Sorry. I was just—"

"Now, now." She wipes her hands on the bottom of her crisp apron. "I won't hear any apologies, young lady. It's not your fault that I'm not used to visitors. It's been quite some time since we've had company." The woman shoos me toward a stool tucked under the corner of the countertop. "Sit. You must be famished."

Bud, the taxi driver, had refused to run me through a drive-thru once he'd picked me up from the hospital, even though I promised to pay him for the ten extra minutes it would take. He'd been overly intent on getting me here with as few stops as possible, though. Thanks to Bud, I haven't eaten more than a small bag of pretzels since dinner last night.

I barely plunk myself down on the stool before the woman swoops in with an overflowing platter of turkey drumsticks and mashed potatoes and gravy garnished with a mound of buttered corn.

"Fankyou," I mumble through my first greedy mouthful.

A warm smile lights up her wrinkled features, and she waves me away with her hand. "No, thank *you*, my dear. I've been waiting for you for ages."

I wouldn't call a couple of weeks *ages*, but whatever.

As I eat, her eyes track my every reaction to her meal. All the attention makes me self-conscious, especially when I dig into the turkey with my hands, but she's so eager to feed me. Everything is so delicious that I don't ask her to stop.

"I'm Millie," she offers, still watching me over the top of her round spectacles.

I gulp down the bite in my mouth. "I'm Lucy."

"You've made me so very happy, Lucy."

No, Millie. You've made me *so very happy.* If I had to choke down what the hospital tried to pass off as food one more day, I would have gone nuts. The meal she's prepared for me surpasses most of the Thanksgiving dinners I can remember, even my Nonna's.

Sorry, Nonna, I think, glancing toward the ceiling. *Your turkey was always too dry. But your tamales made up for it.*

Mille chatters while she scoops vanilla ice cream into a small bowl. "You know, I used to cook for a family—a large family, ten children, oh my!—who didn't have as much as Miss Perdita. We went through some rough times . . . Weeks on end without a crumb to eat."

"That must have been horrible," I reply as I swirl gravy into my mashed potatoes with my fork.

Millie quiets, and I glance up at her. Her hooded eyes brim with tears and her lower lip trembles. "I always regretted not being able to do more to feed those little ones. I should have tried harder . . ." Her voice drifts off.

"Well, I'm sure you did what you could," I say, though I'm not sure what she's talking about. "You sure helped me today. I was starving."

"Do you mean it?" Millie's silver eyebrows shoot upward towards the brim of her bonnet, and she claps her hands. Joy radiates from every inch of her round body, and I can't help but smile.

"Of course I do." I scoop up another bite of potatoes. "Thank you."

When I look up from my plate again, Millie has disappeared, leaving me to finish the rest of my meal in peace.

Maybe Aunt Perdita's wouldn't be so bad with a sweet old cook like Millie around. I can't remember what it's like to have a grandmother care for me, since one of mine passed away before I could remember, and Alzheimer's stole Nonna away from me. Millie seems like the next best thing. I take one more bite of mashed potatoes and close my eyes, willing myself to feel happy.

The next morning, I wake up and set out on my trek to the kitchen, where I pray Mille will have bacon and eggs frying on the stove. Instead, Aunt Perdita greets me with a dark gaze over the brim of her coffee cup. A bowl of cereal sits on the counter in front of her. No eggs or bacon in sight. And no Millie. I fight my disappointment.

"Good morning, Aunt Perdita," I say, even though she clearly doesn't appear to be a morning person. "Where's Millie?"

My aunt slams her mug onto the counter, and I jump at how loudly it rings throughout the kitchen. Yeah, she obviously isn't a morning person. I make a mental note to remember that for tomorrow morning: don't ask Aunt Perdita questions until she finishes her coffee.

"Why are you asking me?" she snarls. "You're the last one to see her."

I wrap my arms around my chest, not liking her sudden display of aggression. "Okay, I have no clue what you're talking about. Millie made me dinner and . . . And then she was gone," I stammer. "I don't know what happened to her."

"Millie's been with me for years, then you show up and she's nowhere to be found," Aunt Perdita spits. "Funny coincidence."

A long row of stark white coffee mugs hangs against the wall next to the coffeemaker. I pretend to take a while selecting my favorite so I can figure out what to say back to her. Once I pull one from its little hook, I grab the carafe, only to discover my aunt hasn't saved any coffee for me. It's only coffee, not the end of the world. But still, her oversight makes me feel even more unwanted by my only family.

Tears well up in my eyes and threaten to spill out. "I didn't do anything. She told me about the family she used to work for and I thanked her for feeding me. That was it," I insist, staring down at the empty carafe in my hands.

Aunt Perdita shuts her eyes and pinches the bridge of her nose with her thin fingers. "You *thanked* her?"

"Yeah, you know. The three magic words—please and thank you. Was that wrong?" This is confusing. Since when were manners a problem?

She places her hands down on either side of her cereal bowl, but they're clenched in fists. "You'd do best to keep your mouth shut."

My mouth falls open in direct violation. The woman who sits before me resembles my mother in all the most obvious ways—her full, flaxen hair; the structure of her cheekbones; those sparkling blue eyes—but my mother never treated me this way, even at my worst teenage moment.

Without another word, I slip the carafe back into its spot on the coffeemaker and rush from the kitchen. If Aunt Perdita wants me to keep my mouth shut, I will.

25

Chapter 3

I don't know where I'm going, only that I can't stand to be in the house with *her* for one more minute. Storming out the front door and slamming it behind me would feel so satisfying, but my dumb leg slows me down so much that my dramatic exit turns out to be pathetic instead.

Norman isn't in the yard when I work my way down the steps to the driveway, and I breathe a sigh of relief. My pulse picks up as I remember the crazy, panicked look in his eyes and the way he'd rattled me around. He'd been so sure I held the answers to something big, something life-changing. Sorry to break it to poor Norman, but I won't be of much help to him. I need answers of my own.

My stomach gurgles impatiently, reminding me that I skipped breakfast in favor of getting as far away from Aunt Perdita as possible. I hadn't paid close attention to the shops near the city square when we drove through yesterday, but there has to be food somewhere. When I reach the end of the drive, I hobble to the left, staying on the sidewalk. My legs are already jelly and beads of sweat dot my brow. This is going to take a while.

Rows of fairly ordinary houses make up this part of Mitte. Vinyl-sided bungalows in faded shades of brown and grey congregate with garish brick ranches and moss-covered wooden A-frames. In comparison to the rest of her neighborhood, Aunt Perdita's place is a castle. She's probably some kind of big deal around here. Big deal or not, it doesn't give her the right to treat me like scum.

As I walk toward the center of town, I keep expecting to see the usual neighborhood activity: people out watering their lawns before the heat of the day, or kids crouched down drawing hopscotch squares on the pavement. But there's nothing. No one jogs past me during a morning workout or lets their dog sniff and relieve themselves on the trees lining the street. Come to think of it, I can't remember hearing a single dog bark a hello as I passed. That alone is really strange.

Just when I begin to wonder if my aunt and I had missed a town evacuation or something, a black cat scurries across the street. It bounds up to a bungalow the shade of a robin's egg and slips inside through a cat door. As I watch the flap of the cat door swing shut once again, something furry bumps against the bare skin of my lower leg. I yelp, and the sound echoes down the still street. A well-fed orange tomcat rubs his chin on my calf, then winds a figure-eight around my legs, purring the whole time. I nudge him away with the toe of my sneaker, and he sneezes in indignation.

"Go on, now," I say. He sinks to his haunches in the center of the sidewalk and blinks at me twice. A block or so down the street, another cat attempts to climb a tree.

No dogs, though. And no birds flitting from tree to tree. I haven't even needed to slap at a nibbling fly. But cats? Oh yeah. There are cats.

Mitte probably has ordinances against dogs. For Spring Break a couple of years ago, I visited my best friend's grandparents in Boca. They live in a community full of shuffleboard lovers. Maybe Mitte's like that, except everyone here is a crazy cat lady. They must have an excellent exterminator, too, to get rid of all the unsightly pests. If my aunt has anything to do with Mitte's operation, I'm sure I'm right. She probably kills everything with her bare hands.

Where are the people who live in the houses, then? My stomach rolls at the thought of being stranded in this ghost town if my hip gives out or I lose my way. I don't even know my aunt's phone number, and even if I did, I lost my cell phone in the car wreck. Maybe I should admit defeat and turn back toward Aunt Perdita's.

Considering my options, I glance back the way I'd come. I can barely make him out, but a man—Norman?—stoops down to prune the bushes around the mansion's massive gate. Coming within a hundred feet of Norman is a worse idea than collapsing on the sidewalk, so I bite my lip and press onward. Someone would give me a lift if I really needed it. I mean, cars are everywhere—resting along the curbs and in some of the driveways. Though I haven't actually seen a vehicle in motion other than Bud's taxi since setting foot in this place, I'll figure out a way back to the mansion if I really need it.

After what seems like hours, I stumble across a diner tucked into the corner of a row of buildings, what must be Mitte's Main Street. I pull open the heavy glass door and walk in, expecting to be the only one there. To my surprise, patrons fill most of the dozen or so booths lined up along the windows. I release my breath, relieved I haven't missed the Rapture after all.

There's an empty spot at the counter. I slide onto the stool between a motorcyclist encased in black leather and chains and an old man who eyes me then shifts his plate away with a gnarled hand.

Because I'd been in a hurry to leave the house, I'd forgotten to wrap my head to hide the series of long scarlet scars running from the top of my head to the middle of my forehead. The scarf I wear each day makes me less self-conscious about it until my hair grows back in and covers the damage. I assume my patchwork of flesh frightened the old man, and shield my forehead with my fingers. I'd be frightened of me, too, if I didn't know my own story.

A gum-popping woman with an impossibly high mound of black hair on her head sashays up to me. She drops a smudged menu in front of me.

"Hey, sugar. Whatcha drinkin'?" Her words squeeze straight out of her nostrils.

I unfold the menu and scan their breakfast offerings. "Water, please."

"You got it." Off she sways to grab my drink. She returns impossibly fast, glass in hand. "Know what you want?"

Looking at the menu had been pointless. The idea of Millie's eggs and bacon is stuck in my mind, so that's what I order.

Halfway through my omelet, I remember something else I've forgotten. My money.

The restaurant bustles with customers, and I debate on the likelihood of being caught if I try to skip out on my bill. In the end, though, I talk myself out of it. Everyone would know the awful thing I'd done, and in a town as tiny as Mitte someone would recognize me almost immediately. That isn't really the kind of first impression I'd hoped to make. So I do the only thing I can think of.

"Hey," I call to the waitress the next time she looks in my direction. She grins, showing off a row of teeth that contrast sharply against her shiny pink lipstick, and moves toward me.

She sashays over. "What's up, hon?"

The words stick in my throat and my cheeks burn until I finally blurt, "I don't have any money."

If my confession stuns her, she doesn't show it. Her jaws keep up a steady pace, chewing away on her ancient piece of bubble gum. I wait for her to cuss me out or call the police. When she doesn't, I prepare myself for an afternoon slaving away over a sink brimming with dirty dishes.

Instead, she pats me on the arm and smiles. I mean, *really smiles*. "Don't you worry, sweetie. Let me take care of that." She moves a few paces to the window that opens into the kitchen. "Hey, Sal."

"Yeah? What is it?" A burly man with thick black hair peppered with greys peers through the slot in the window. He looks out of place here in the diner. It's easier to see him in a pin-striped suit, fedora, and machine gun. He looks like the kind of guy who would much rather fit me with a custom pair of cement shoes than forgive my debt.

The waitress drops her voice as she fills Sal in on my predicament. Sal pinches his forehead between fingers the size of hot dogs. My brain signals my feet to get ready to run—or hop, whatever—and I shift to the side of my stool. My knees bump the old man in the thigh, and he growls obscenities at me.

"Sorry," I mumble.

Her voice drifts back to me. "Okay, okay, Sal. We'll work it out. Keep your shirt on!"

Sweat begins to pool just above my upper lip, and I close my eyes, sorry I ran away without a plan. At the very least, I should have thought it through well enough to grab the essentials: my cash and my disguise.

The waitress returns to me. Her gaze rests on her clasped hands as her gleaming teeth bite gently on the corner of her lower lip.

"Listen, hon. I've done some things I ain't very proud of. This one time, I took money from Carla Giametti's purse. It was right there, stickin' outta the top of that fancy purse of hers. Served her right, I thought to myself."

"But I'm not steal—"

She silences me with her hand. "What I didn't know was that she was tryin' to save up money to leave that no-good Danny of hers. She needed that money more than I did."

For the life of me, I can't imagine why she feels the need to tell me all of this, but I listen politely. My only other option is a very slow and awkward getaway.

"I'm gonna go back there right now and tell Sal to take your meal from my paycheck. Consider it my treat." She pauses, then adds, "It's the least I can do. For Carla."

I deflate a little at her generosity. "That's so nice of you . . . Uh, I didn't get your name."

Her eyes twinkle as she taps her name badge with a hot pink fingernail. "It's Vera."

A name tag, of course. I never notice that kind of thing. "Vera," I correct myself. "Thank you so much. I'll pay you back, I swear. I'll go get—"

"Don't be silly." Her face lights up. Beneath that mountain of hair and spackle on her face, Vera is beautiful—and I'm not just saying that because she'd saved me from sleeping with the fish.

"Thank you, then."

Our eyes meet. "No. Thank you, Lucy."

She knows my name even though I'd made it a point to keep that info to myself.

These creepy small towns, I think, but I keep my smile pasted in place until Vera bumps open the swinging door to the kitchen with her hip.

"Oh Sal . . ." she sings. Then her voice hushes, and I can't hear her anymore.

The energy in the restaurant changes like the flip of a light switch. The normal buzz of conversation dies down, and the heat of a dozen pairs of eyes turns on me. I'd missed something major.

Before I can figure out what happened, Sal storms through the swinging door. Patches of red stand out on his cheeks. "Out."

I look around, feeling embarrassed for the poor target of his wrath. Sal's kind of a scary guy.

He stabs the air in my direction with the spatula in his fist, then points towards the main entrance. "No, *you*. Get out!"

Even though I'm confused and want to ask him what the problem is, I trust my instincts. Time to leave before Sal starts chucking things at me in blind rage.

As I thump quickly to the door, Sal grumbles, "Where'm I gonna find another waitress? Stupid girl . . ."

Out on the sidewalk, I can feel their eyes. Even though the windows obscure everyone inside the diner from my view, I know they're still watching. Goosebumps prickle on my arms and intuition tugs at me again, eager to get back to the mansion. I hate that mansion and I hate my aunt, but at least my room is a haven from the creepiness of Mitte.

Before I finish crossing the street, a gruff voice yells out to me from outside the diner. "Hey!"

He means me, no question about it, but I act like I don't hear.

Step-thump-step-thump-step-thump. I concentrate on putting one foot in front of the other then repeating the awful process.

Heavy footfalls chase me from behind. I whirl around to face him. A wave of nausea rolls through me at my careless movement, but I fight to focus. This time my predator is not my pain, it's the man dressed in black leather and chains.

He doesn't blend in well here, with mirrored shades covering his eyes and a wiry red beard trailing down to his chest. A tattoo of a skull on fire—a skull! On fire!—peeks out from under the cuff of his black t-shirt. The man's only reassuring feature is the bandana covering his head, but I'm mostly jealous. The late morning sun makes my scar feel too hot and exposed.

"I'm talking to you, girl." He curls his upper lip. When he takes in my wide eyes and frightened posture, he softens. "Stop looking at me like that. I ain't going to hurt you."

I find little comfort in his words, but I draw in a breath to steady my racing heart. "Ohhhhh-kay . . . Can I help you?"

He swivels his thick neck to look over his shoulder, then back at me. "Who *are* you?"

My parents taught me never to talk to strangers. This is a new town, though. In Mitte, *I* am the stranger.

"I'm Perdita's niece. I just moved here," I say.

His expression changes. "Listen, I don't need no life story, cupcake. Who you know or where you came from—that don't matter. All I wanna know is what happened to Vera."

"How should I know?"

"But you gotta know. It has somethin' to do with you." Desperation colors his tone. The veins on each side of his wide, sunburned neck pop out.

A small group of fellow diners have filtered from the restaurant, watching us from the sidewalk. My gaze flits past the biker and back before I shrug. "I'm sorry."

The man heaves a great sigh and takes a step back. It seems like a good time for me to make my retreat, so I urge myself forward. He will catch me easily if he takes a few long strides, but I don't dare look backwards. I don't want to know if I am being followed.

After a long while, the mansion comes into view. Summoning my last ounce of energy, I drag myself up the stone steps and to my room. I don't bother showering at all, and instead burrow beneath the down comforter in my room.

These four walls are my only safety.

Chapter 4

I spend the next day exploring the mansion, careful to avoid my aunt. It's easy to figure out when she's awake and moving throughout the house because she makes a lot of noise. Especially when she bangs around in the kitchen like a *poltergeist*.

My room is in the south wing. I count thirteen white doors in my hallway, all closed. When I try the doorknobs, about half of them are locked. A few of the unlocked rooms are clear of furniture, just an expanse of bare hardwood surrounded by blank white walls. In each of the empty rooms, the sheer drapes have been pulled across the windows in a pointless attempt to keep others from peering in. The furnished rooms are set up identically to mine. They are all too bright and sterile, not unlike the hospital.

I wait until my aunt retreats to her room before I gather the nerve to open the heavy door in the foyer. I expect something sinister—a dungeon, perhaps, or a sweatshop. When I slide the paneled door to the side, instead of toddler seamstresses or stretching racks, all I find is a row of overinflated red-upholstered couches. Those couches might be considered sinister, I guess. I know they're liars, at least, not nearly as comfortable as they appear. On both sides of the room, books of every shape and size spill from floor-to-ceiling shelves. I resist the urge to plop down on one of the rock-hard loveseats with a musty old novel in favor of venturing deeper into the space.

Four gigantic panes of glass comprise the far wall, with a set of French doors nestled within them. Beyond the windows stretches my own personal Garden of Eden.

I glance over my shoulder to make sure I'm still alone, then I ease the door open and step outside. The breeze wraps around my body, lifting the loose tail of my head scarf and sending it, tickling, across the nape of my neck.

The stone patio beneath my feet arcs in the shape of a crescent moon. I picture large parties here under the stars, with a live band and colorful lanterns strung about. If that is the sort of thing that takes place, I find no evidence of it, not even the tiniest of patio tables or a wilted lawn chair. *Aunt Perdita, you party pooper.*

The green velvet of the lawn trickles down until it fades into the dancing shade of the trees beyond. The fragrance of the fruit among the branches wraps around me with the next crescendo of wind. It draws me in, and I move quietly into the shadowy arms of the orchard.

Surrounded by trees, I feel at peace for the first time since driving into this crazy podunk town. It doesn't make sense, because being in the middle of nowhere, away from the comforting background noises of the city, usually makes me anxious. It was the reason my parents had to drive three hours in the middle of the night to pick me up from summer camp when I was ten. Here, though, I don't feel the usual panic. Among the thick carpet of grass, sparkling with beams of sunlight filtering through the leaves, I feel whole. Despite my limp, I weave my way among the maze of tree trunks, immersing myself in this new place.

I'm not sure how long I wander before the orchard thins out and slopes downward and out of sight. Traversing the hill isn't easy but, really, nothing is anymore. Out here, at least I don't have to worry about Aunt Perdita and her mood swings, or the psycho inhabitants of my new town.

Near the foot of the hill, a weathered split-rail fence forms a boundary. On the other side of the fence, bushes full of roses of all different shades grow. Not seeing a gate or gap into the thicket, I stuff myself into the opening between the splintered rails. My bad leg doesn't cooperate when I ask it to bend, but with a bit of coaxing I ease my way to the other side.

A dirt path, dark and slick with late-day condensation, leads into the center of the greenery. I follow it with hesitation, certain I must be trespassing on someone's property. But the perfume from the blossoms pushes a memory to the forefront, clouding my good sense.

Pink roses had always been mom's favorite. Dad used to bring her a freshly-cut pink rose every Friday. She would act surprised, as if he'd never done it before, then reach up on her tiptoes to kiss him. Afterwards, she would prune the stem down until it was just the head of the flower and release it in a crystal vase half-full of water.

Always a pink rose. Always the shared kiss. Always, and perhaps most importantly, the surprised joy.

A lump forms in my throat before I can brace myself against it. I bring my hand to my forehead and squeeze my eyes shut, physically trying to quell my tears. The whole thing happened because of me. I don't deserve to feel sorry for myself, to cry.

Behind me, in the direction of the path, a twig snaps. Such a small thing out here in nature, except I remember the whole trespassing thing. My imagination jumps into overdrive. Uncertain of who or what lurks towards me, my sadness flashes into a surge of adrenaline. I swing my head around, ignoring the bolt of fire in my neck. That path stands as my only way out unless I want to fight and bleed my way through the rose bushes, and I most definitely don't.

"Look what we have here. A rose of unspeakable beauty amongst the thorns." Oliver smiles, tipping the brim of his brown fedora as he steps into view.

My heart beats again. "I'm so glad it's you. You have no idea."

"Lucy, you *do* care about me, after all." He laughs and his dark eyes sparkle. "I knew it."

"'Care for you' is such a strong statement, but so far you're the only one I've met in Mitte that (a) I've seen more than once, and (b) hasn't been a complete sociopath." I turn to follow him as he sidles past me and closer to the flowers.

He pulls a pair of small scissors from the pocket of his trousers and busies himself with cutting away the spent blooms. "I could be a sociopath, you know," he says, pausing long enough to arch his eyebrow at me.

"Yeah, you do seem pretty shady, now that I think of it."

Oliver chuckles. "And, for the record, they're not sociopaths. The people here are—" He looks off into the distance as he handpicks the perfect descriptive word. "—troubled."

Perfect. "Troubled, how?" Though I really don't want to know the answer. He doesn't offer one.

"Rumor is you met Angus yesterday."

"Angus? The sasquatch in all the leather?" I sink down to the earth to rest my aching leg.

"That's the one," Oliver says.

"If by 'met' you mean 'was hunted down by,' then, yep, I met him."

His hands move quickly and without faltering, like he's memorized every vine. If the thorns rip at his flesh, he never once complains. He remains quiet a long while, until I forget what we'd been talking about. The woods around us fall silent, too, except the snip-snip of Oliver's shears as he works.

"Sal's pretty upset by Vera leaving," he says, finally. "You probably should avoid him for a while."

I groan and pinch a blade of grass from the soil. "I didn't do anything. I keep telling everyone."

Oliver pitches a withered bud to the ground and turns to me. "It would also be a really good idea if you didn't go exploring around town on your own. I'm not sure it's safe."

I study his face for any hint of joking, but find none. Oliver and I barely know each other, but I guess he isn't serious very often. His smile is gone and my blood chills within my veins.

I pry my eyes from him and stare at my lap, not sure what to say. If he's concerned, maybe I should be, too. Oliver seems to know everything about my strange new home, so what if there really is something or someone out there I should be wary of? Then again, everything about him screams old-fashioned, from his wool pants and suspenders to his ideals. I consider the possibility that women aren't treated as equals in Mitte. My mind conjures up the image of him lugging my suitcase up the front stairs for me because, as a woman, I lack the strength to manage it myself. A flash of anger streaks through me and I struggle to stand.

Oliver notices my flopping and groaning, and steps to me with hand outstretched. "Here, let me help."

I slap him away. "I can do it myself."

A look of confusion settles upon his features. "Lucy, I never said you couldn't."

I ignore him until I make it to my feet. The effort of standing nearly incapacitates me, but I refuse to let him know. Instead, I grit my teeth. "Stop treating me like a child."

The words echo inside of me. *Stop treating me like a child.* I crash to my knees, all the energy it took to stand wasted.

Crash . . .

Dad sits in the back seat. My mother barks worried instructions from my side.

"Lucy. LUCY, SLOW DOWN!" she screeches, digging her fingernails into the vinyl seat.

I shoot her an irritated look over my shoulder, defying all I've ever learned in Driver's Ed. "Chill out, Mom. I know! Stop treating me like a child."

"The road, Luce!" Dad bellows. I catch the whites of his eyes before I snap my gaze forward.

It's too late. My knuckles blanch white on the steering wheel. My body braces for impact.

Chapter 5

I bolt upright in bed, my clothes plastered to my body with sweat. I'd been dreaming, but about what, I can't remember. Something was a dream. Something was reality.

More than anything, I want the crash to have been a horrible dream. I want to open my eyes and be whole again. I want my parents to be in the other room, sleeping peacefully under their covers. I don't want to accept them as dead and gone, sleeping eternally under the cover of earth. I want to be with them, as I should be. I squeeze my eyes shut against the tears.

My conversation with Oliver in the rose garden didn't make an ounce of sense, and it seems more like the nonsense dreams are usually made of. He'd made it clear there's reason for me to be cautious in Mitte, and that my neighbors all have issues. I'm sure the "issues" part includes my lovely aunt. If my safety is questionable within the mansion, Oliver never clued me in. Guess I'll just have to watch my back.

This place just keeps getting better and better.

The sky remains light beyond my curtains, allowing me to make out the sparse furniture in my room. There's something very disorienting about Mitte, and I'm sure entire days could be lost here without even realizing it. I turn to look over my shoulder at the bedside stand and, again, the absence of an alarm clock ticks me off. I make a mental note to buy one next time I summon the bravery to venture downtown.

Instead of being greeted by the time, a single pink rose floats inside a clear vase on the table. My breath catches in my throat, and I scuttle backward until there's nowhere to go but to my feet. No one knows about the rose except for my parents. I'd never told a soul, especially in this Godforsaken town. But, yet, someone obviously knows.

A pink rose, every week. Always floating in the bowl. A pink rose.

Oliver.

I don't know where to find him, but I head to the last place I saw him. Despite the inky light of dusk, I creep in the direction of the rose garden, tripping a few times on twisted roots along the way. The orchard stretches on without end. After a while the darkness deepens, curling around me like a thick black fog. I stumble again and reach out to steady myself on anything within grasp, which happens to be a gnarled tree trunk. On my feet again, I move forward into the blackness.

My bravery is rewarded by the ankle of my good leg twisting sideways in a rut, depositing me onto the dew-soaked earth. I don't need to put weight on my ankle to know I twisted it; the pulsing pain radiating from my heel to midway up my calf tells me as much. Rolling to my hands and knees, I inch my way forward until my fingertips meet the spidery pedestal of the next tree. As soon as I drag myself close enough, I turn to prop my back against the tree and wait for daylight. This isn't even remotely a plan, but it's all I have.

My clothes from earlier are no match for the night's humidity. In the absence of sleeves, I curl my arms around my chest and pull my bent knees towards me. With any luck, any wandering mosquitos will ignore my bare flesh until the morning sun arrives. That goes double for any lurking, bloodthirsty creatures of the night. The more I worry about the things I can't see—which, at this point, is everything—the more I realize something more disturbing. No crickets chirp their shrill concerto. No bats sing out as they swoop through the dark. No unknown vermin scurry through the greenery around me. Nature isn't meant to have a mute button, and prickles begin at the flesh on my wrists and spread upward.

My hearing focuses as much as possible beyond the slight buzz in my left ear from when my head smacked the windshield. Nothing beyond the ruffling of the breeze through the apple trees. Once, I heard something fall, and I brushed it off as an apple plummeting to the ground. Other than that, it's almost as if the orchard exists in a void.

I don't know how long I sit there, trembling from a mixture of fear and the cold. I'm so thoroughly creeped out that any amount of time is too long. Tears well up in my eyes and I let myself cry into my knees. I wish I would have died in that crash after all. If I'd died, I wouldn't be stuck in this awful place wondering what's wrong with everyone, why my aunt hates my guts, and where all the noise has gone. Death won't give me any riddles. Death will give me peace.

"What are you doing out here?" he whispers, breaking the silence.

I let loose with a scream, which splits my skull into about twenty fragments. With my heart nearly bursting in fright, my skull is the very least of my worries. I leap to my feet, the fastest movement I've made in a long time, and whirl to locate the disembodied voice that had spoken from the gloom. Strong hands cup my elbows, but I still can't make out a body, no less a face. With every remaining ounce of fight left, I shove myself away from his grasp, shrieking again and again.

"Shhh, Lucy. Keep it down, would ya?"

I curse my stupid eyes for not being able to pierce the darkness. Whoever *he* is, he certainly isn't having as much trouble seeing me. A hand claps across my mouth, muffling yet another of my screams.

"Hey," he hisses. From the way the word puffs around my nostrils, his face clearly hovers nearby. "Hey, it's Oliver. Stop before they hear you!"

I choke back my next cry, his hand still resting over my lips.

After a moment of my silence, his fingers relax slightly. "You're not going to scream again, are you?" I shake my head slowly, my lips brushing against the calluses he'd earned through years of hard work. His hand falls away back into the blackness.

"Oliver, you scared me to death," I gasp. Though I keep my voice low, I can't disguise the trembling.

He hushes me again. He's still incredibly close. "You're not safe out here by yourself after dark," he whispers. It sounds like he's glancing around.

The urgency in his voice stirs up my earlier fear. "What? What do you mean?"

"I can't tell you what I mean—I would if I could, honest. You've just got to trust me on this."

"I was trying to find you."

"You came out here for me?"

"Yeah. To tell you thank you." I hesitate. "And to ask how you knew about the whole rose thing."

He doesn't answer right away, and I fear he's left me all alone again. The thought of being alone, especially after he'd sounded so concerned, sends a shiver through me.

"You're cold. Let's get you back to the house."

"I can't walk. My ankle's twisted." I shift my weight forward to confirm.

"Can you ride?"

"Excuse me?"

"Can. You. Ride?" he repeats. "My horse is around here somewhere."

A horse? Even though the darkness continues to veil everything from view, I scan the area for the presence of another living being. Still nothing.

"I'm scared of horses," I confess, blushing. At least he can't see how embarrassed I am. "One bucked me off when I was younger."

Maybe it's my imagination, but I think I hear him stifle a laugh.

"It's not funny," I say, and it really isn't. That pony had been demonic, dumping me in the dirt and then trotting off the trail to munch on dandelions.

"No, no. I'm not laughing at you." The grin is evident in his tone. *Jerk.*

Oliver whistles as softly as the rush of wind through blades of grass.

My stomach churns in dread. "Can we skip the horse?"

A few seconds later, something nuzzles the palm of my hand as it dangles at my side. It takes everything within me to keep from crying out again.

"Jasper!" Oliver chuckles. "Where are your manners? She doesn't have any treats."

A peace offering.

I nudge around with my toe until I locate a fallen apple. I crouch down, hoping the horse won't kick me in the face, and pick it up.

"Here, Jasper." I stretch my hand outward, offering the piece of fruit to the blackness.

The velvet of a muzzle shifts across my palm, tickling my skin. Then the apple pushes against my hand before it's crunched in half. A being stands in front of me with jaws strong enough to make applesauce from my offering, and I can't even see it. Kind of unnerving.

"I wish I could see you guys," I whisper as Jasper mouths the rest of the apple out of my hand.

The smile in Oliver's voice disintegrates. "No, you don't."

Oliver is especially mysterious tonight. He probably wants to freak me out like those little boys at summer camp. Those boys laughed when their spooky fireside stories made me beg to call my parents.

Boys. They never grow up.

"Do you trust me?" he asks. He's closer to me.

"Do I have a choice?"

"Not really. We've got to get you back to the mansion before . . ." His voice trails off. I want to slug him in the arm for being spooky again, but I'd have to find his arm first.

He swoops in without warning, whisking me from my feet. Again, I cry out. He sucks in a sharp breath that catches between his teeth. "Lucy, I'm not kidding—stop making noise."

My blood simmers beneath my skin. "Warn me next time you're planning on picking me up, then."

"Sorry," he fires back, his mouth too close to my ear.

I want nothing more than for the strength in my legs to return so I can get away from him and his nerve, but Oliver is in control now and holds me pressed unnecessarily tightly to his body. Turning my head from him is my only means of escape. *I'd shown him, all right.*

With a little more energy than necessary, he heaves me up into the blackness. My bottom connects to something soft yet solid—Jasper's back—and pain spikes down my spine. I gasp as my body starts to curl in on itself.

"Okay," Oliver says. "Slide your right leg over to the other side. I'll keep you steady."

My mouth flops open and I wonder if he can see the ever-growing whites of my eyes. Or maybe he's picked up on the stampede going on between the valves of my heart, because he softens. "Lucy, I'm not going to let you fall. Trust me."

"The only people I've ever trusted are dead," I shoot down to him as I claw around for something, anything, to keep me from falling on my face.

Oliver snorts, which sends me over the edge.

"What? You think that's funny?" I challenge him, no longer concerned about keeping quiet. His hand clamps on my leg in piercing reproof. I'll have bruises there tomorrow, for sure. Through locked teeth, I order, "Let. Go."

"Please stop," he says. "I'm trying to keep you sa—"

A rumble beyond us, where the orchard fades into the rest of the forest, interrupts his plea. Even though I sit astride stoic Jasper, I can feel the ground vibrating beneath us.

"What in the—?" I cry, whipping my head in the direction of the growing commotion.

"Slide back," Oliver commands. I know better than to take offense at his bossy tone. I'd made a big mistake, one he'd been trying to protect me from. The fear of horses leaves my body, only to be replaced by the fear of the unknown. Ignoring the bite of pain in my hip, I throw my leg over Jasper's withers and shove myself backward, using my palms for leverage. A second later, Oliver sweeps himself upward and in front of me on his horse's back.

"Hold on," he yells over the thunder moving our direction. I hug my body to his and wrap my arms around his middle like my life depends on it, because I'm pretty sure it does.

Our mount launches forward without waiting for Oliver's cue, galloping forward into the gloom. The surge of movement pitches me to the side, and I dig my heels into Jasper's side trying to right myself. The horse lashes back at me, gnashing my foot between his teeth.

"Jasper!" Oliver barks, spurring him along.

Jasper releases my foot and races forward, but not before kicking up his back heels in protest. In case I'd forgotten, this lovely creature reminds me of why I loathe horses. I close my eyes tight and clutch Oliver with all my remaining strength.

By the rush of air tickling my bare scalp, I know we're flying. I can't think about any of it— the scream of the wind in my ears, the sting of branches as they slice into my flesh, how a fall from this speed would probably finish the job the car crash hadn't. With each terrifying stride, my heart nears explosion. I do the only thing I can think to do in the situation: I bury my head into Oliver's back and pray. Though I suspect God isn't listening, I have to try.

The great noise draws closer, like a freight train plowing through the stillness. A prickle of goosebumps starts low on my spine and travels upward despite the night air turning hot and bitter. "What is it?" I shout, but Oliver doesn't hear me or doesn't bother with a reply.

Do they have bears out here? Mountain lions? Angry apple farmers with pitchforks? If this is the peaceful country living I've heard so much about all my life, I want the city back. In the city, street lights glow on every corner. There, you can usually see danger before it claws you in the back. The only thing visible here is a pinpoint of light dancing between the arms of the trees. That faint glow grows, and as it does I feel the murmur of hope. Civilization isn't that far off. Maybe I won't die after all.

"Be ready. When we stop, *run*," Oliver says. "Get inside."

I squeeze harder with my arms around his middle in acknowledgement. We're almost to the house, the border of the orchard about a hundred yards off. All I need to do is make it across the patio and lock myself inside the house. It all seems so easy, until I remember my twisted ankle. I can barely walk, let alone run. I open my mouth to remind Oliver, but the words never make it out.

A flash of red ignites beyond the tree line. It settles directly in our path, separating us from safety. Jasper whinnies then wheels upward and onto his hind legs. With nothing to hold onto other than Oliver, I feel myself slipping. Gripping with my knees doesn't slow me. We tumble backward from the horse's back.

"Jasper, nooo!" Oliver cries just before landing on top of me. The weight of his body crushes my ribcage. I lose consciousness.

Chapter 6

My eyes flutter open. My daily assault from the glaring white of my bedroom walls. I close them again.

"Lucy, you awake?" I recognize Oliver's voice.

My arms rest at my sides. I tap my index finger, the best response I can manage; everything else sets my body ablaze with pain so intense that bile rises in my throat. At least fifty questions about our getaway pop into my brain, but the words dry up in my parched mouth. I don't ask for water to help me speak, though. Deep down, I know I'm not strong enough to hear the truth.

His footsteps cross my bedroom, and then my door opens. He calls down the hallway, "Hey, Doc. She's come 'round."

Oliver's voice ricochets in my ears, sending shockwaves through my skull. I want to throw things at him to shut him up, but the ache in my chest advises against it. Instead, I manage a feeble "Stopit" through my clenched teeth.

The door creaks shut, and he returns to my bedside. "Sorry about that. Doc Blevins wanted to know when you woke up."

"How long?" I moan, pulling my heavy eyelids open with great effort.

Oliver settles in a chair next to me. "How long what?"

"I passed out," I say. "How long ago?"

He brings his hand to his forehead and rubs it. His forehead is wrapped in a white bandage. A crimson splotch has begun to soak through above his right ear.

My eyes widen. Only the pain keeps me from bolting upright in bed. "Oliver, your head!" But it isn't only his head. The hollow of his left eye has turned purple-black, and his eye is red where it should be white. Blood trickles from the corner of his mouth. "You're hurt."

Oliver hushes me, reaching out his hand to stroke my forehead. I flinch and pull back when his thumb grazes over my scar.

"Sorry, I didn't mean to—"

"My scarf." My eyes dart around the room in search of the familiar sheath of fabric. "Where's my scarf?"

His mouth drops open in surprise. The dark blood at the corner of his mouth runs to his chin. He doesn't seem to notice it. "Maybe it fell off in the orchard when the . . ." He looks away without finishing his sentence. "I'll find it, promise."

His promises don't help me now, though. I pinch my eyelids closed, remembering how I used to play hide-and-seek as a child. Cowering in plain sight, chubby hands covering my dark eyes, so certain I'd chosen the perfect hiding place because the seeker was invisible. Maybe if I can't see Oliver, he can't see me, right? The car accident not only took away everything I loved, but it left things behind, too. Scars. Twisted roadmaps to the handful of surgeries I had under my belt. My dark hair now grows in uneven patches, skipping over the sutures completely. I don't want anyone to notice my brokenness. I cover what cracks and breaks I can with pretty silk scarves. But Oliver sees me. And he sees through my disguise.

"What are you so afraid of?"

"I'm not afraid," I snap, opening my eyes to glare at him.

"You don't need that old scarf, Luce."

"Like you know what I need. What *you* need is a doctor or something before you get blood all over my stuff." I try to pull my blanket out of his splash zone, but the movement causes me to groan. Concern clouds Oliver's face as he leans in closer to comfort me. I recoil. "Your mouth!"

Oliver swipes the corner of his lips, and his eyes widen at the smear of red on his fingertips. "I'm sorry. I didn't want you to see me like this, but I . . . I couldn't leave you."

"I'm sure my aunt would have taken care of me," I lie. The woman doesn't possess a single maternal bone in her body.

"Well, no. That's not likely." He fishes a handkerchief from the deep pocket of his trousers and dabs his mouth. "Miss Perdita isn't what I'd call a night owl. Fact of the matter is, no one around Mitte is, really. That's why I was saying you shouldn't be wandering about in the middle of the night all by yourself."

"I was doing fine until you scared me to death."

He snorts. "If you call freezing in the middle of an orchard fine, then, yep. You were doin' just fine."

"And then your horse nearly killed us both. See why I hate them?"

Oliver grimaces. "Jasper promised he wouldn't do that again. I'm so sorry. He's really scared of—"

"He promised? You *talk* to your horse?" I can't hide the acid in my voice. "You're insane."

He remains silent, but his bloodied lips part at my accusation. The hurt is obvious in his eyes, but I don't feel the least bit sorry for what I said.

I turn my head away from Oliver and close my eyes again, overwhelmed by pain and the craziness of my new town. Back home, I'd never felt so unwelcomed or frightened. How I wish I could turn time back to prevent the crash, or at least try harder to stay with my parents as they made their way to the afterlife. These thoughts bring tears to my eyes.

"I should have died in the crash," I mutter. A tear slides down the side of my nose until it shivers at the tip and falls to the pillow.

Oliver pauses on his way to my bedroom door. "Don't ever say that," he whispers.

I pretend not to hear him. Soon the door squeaks open and closes with a soft click. I'm alone, just like I'd wanted. The room falls silent at once, and I find myself staring at the door, waiting for him to return. As if I hadn't questioned his mental capacity or complained about him bleeding on Aunt Perdita's down comforter. As if I hadn't been a huge jerk.

My life isn't a chick flick, surprise surprise. Oliver doesn't burst through my door, roses in hand, willing to forgive my crankiness because I'm so adorable. No, the only person who bothers visiting at all over the next couple of days is Doc Blevins, and only to flash a penlight at my pupils and slip his frigid stethoscope under my t-shirt. He's pleasant enough, but maybe it's because he looks like a middle-aged Santa Claus, before he turned all snowy white and fluffy in the middle.

By day three, I'm desperate enough for company that I attempt small talk with the doctor. "So, how long have you lived in Mitte? Your whole life?"

Doc finishes securing the ACE bandage protecting my ribs. "Not my whole life, no. You know, I don't rightly recall how long I've been here. Could be a year, could be twenty or more. I don't keep track."

His reply strikes me as odd, but I brush it away because I honestly don't care about the question or his answer. I just want him to stay with me. Instead of feeling guilty about my lack of interest in Doc's history, I skip directly to a topic I find more riveting. "What about Oliver? What's his story?"

Doc's eyes hide behind his wrinkled lids as he grins. "Oliver's a good kid. Showed me around when I first got here."

"So he's, like, the Mitte Welcoming Committee or something?"

"Nah. Nothing like that. We don't see a whole lot of new faces, that's all. We're all drawn to him, one way or another. I think it's because he has something most of us have lost somewhere along the way."

"What's that?"

"Hope."

I snort but it comes out a shaky exhale instead. "Hope? For what?"

Doc smiles down at me, but the smile doesn't disguise his melancholy. "Don't you worry about that, young lady."

I try to push up to sitting so I can fire off more questions, but the stabbing pain in my chest sucks the air right from my lungs. Tears spring to my eyes and I sink back into my pillow.

Doc pats my hand. "There, there. You've been through quite a shock." With a groan and sharp pop of his joints, he rises to his feet.

That's an understatement. Yes, I'd been through a shock, though I can't quite remember what it was. Doc doesn't seem to notice my confusion as I watch him fumble around in his black leather doctor's bag. To everyone else in this Godforsaken town, this mysterious life is normal. They know the rules to get along here, while I stir up trouble every time I do anything. I really need a Mitte handbook or something.

As soon as the black and silver stethoscope is secure with the rest of his things, Doc shuts the bag and turns toward the door.

My pulse picks up pace. He's planning on leaving me alone again. I'd been alone for days, ever since I'd regained consciousness and upset Oliver. In the hospital, the nurses had milled about and asked me questions even if they never expected me to respond. Here I have nothing but blinding white walls and the sound of the wind brushing the shrubs against my window. There's not even the hypnotic *tick-tock* of a clock to lull me to sleep.

Alone is what I thought I wanted to be, but I'm so lonely I'd even welcome a visit from Aunt Perdita.

Doc strides to the door.

"Don't," I rasp. My eyes shine wide and wild.

He pauses, his hand on the doorknob. "What is it, child?"

"Can't you stay a little while?"

Doc shakes his head. "I'm afraid not, Lucy. I've still got another patient to see."

A surge of panic races through my veins, and my body betrays me by trembling. A few days ago, I wanted nothing more than to fade into the background, anonymous and boring, so I wouldn't have to talk about my past or myself. I guess I should be careful what I wish for.

The older man approaches the side of my bed and grazes my upper arm with his fingertips, preparing to abandon me in the madness of the black hole of this room. I flinch at his touch on my bare skin.

"It's getting late, but I'll tell Oliver you'd like some company tomorrow. How 'bout that?"

Yes! "No!"

Doc puts his hand up in surrender. "Fine. I think you could do each other some good. But that's an old man's opinion, and it's worth about as much as you paid for it."

I turn my head away. He's going to leave, and I don't want to watch it happen because I don't know if I'll see another person again until he checks on me next, whenever that is. In the hospital, I'd spent entire days trying to wish away the nurses as they fiddled with machines and tubes. I hated them when they forced me to limp to the bathroom or down the hall, smiling and cheering me on the whole time. Like I'd done any of it because I'd had any kind of choice. When I found out I was moving in with my aunt, I had pictured hours of sleep uninterrupted by beeping monitors or slamming doors at 3 a.m. I dreamed of a world where I didn't have to talk to other people because, clearly, God wanted me to be by myself. But then I set foot in this dumb town and the whole place has turned out to be so unspeakably creepy. The worst thing I can imagine is being alone in Mitte.

The doctor's steps fall away from me as he retreats toward my door. The groan of the hinges causes me to shudder under my blankets, but pride keeps me from begging Doc to stay.

The door doesn't shut right away, and Doc sighs after a couple of seconds. "I'll keep you company a little bit longer, just this once, if you promise me you'll go to sleep."

I don't turn toward him, but he must see my shoulders droop in relief. He shuffles back to my bedside and settles in the chair there.

"Lucy, you should get used to being by yourself. We all have to, you know."

Chapter 7

Sunlight streams through my curtains, blazing a path right through my eyelids. Whoever decided see-through curtains were the way to go on home décor needs a slap upside their head. I can't even change clothes in my own room for fear of omnipresent Oliver, or Norman, the groundskeeper, seeing something they can't unsee. Stupid curtains. Stupid Oliver nosing around in places he doesn't belong so I can't walk around my room in my underwear. Lounging in my skivvies rates near the very bottom of things I normally care about, but, darnit, I find it annoying that he took the option right off the table.

I turn from the blinding light and stare at the door, willing Oliver to walk through with a breakfast-laden tray, an apology for being so infuriating. After what seems like hours of staring, I blow out a breath. There will be no bacon-scented apologies today, not that I want that.

Okay, I sort of want that, because *bacon.*

But mostly, I want company.

Doc had been good company. I surprise myself by feeling sad when I wake up to the empty chair next to my bed. He had slipped out of my room sometime after I drifted off, lulled asleep by his stories of growing up on the golden shores of California.

I dream of water lapping against the sand and a bonfire flickering in the night. Familiar faces surround me—Mom, Dad, Nonna, my best friend Tanya, my track coach Ms. Byers, and even Oliver. Sparks fly up from the smoldering embers, fading into the canopy of stars as we laugh together. My mother holds my father's hand as they look at each other with smiling eyes. Nonna sits next to me on our driftwood bench, her gray head bent over her knitting, a pair of petal pink booties for a baby I've never met. Tanya and Ms. Byers joke around, probably about something that had happened during practice. When I turn my focus to Oliver, he meets my gaze across the flames. The corners of his mouth twitch upward, stirring something unfamiliar in the pit of my stomach. My cheeks burn, and I'm thankful to be able to blame their glow on the heat of the fire.

As I glance from face to face, a long-absent warmth fills my chest until I feel like I might explode from it all. This is the most complete I've been in months. I feel comfortable. I feel happy. I feel loved. I feel hope.

And then, just as it had in real life, reality pushes its way back into my brain. Alone and hopeless again, all I can do is accept it and wake up.

My stomach growls, and I try to remember what I'd eaten the day before. It hadn't been much, only enough to settle my stomach so I could take something for the pain. Last time, Doc brought me a fresh loaf of cinnamon bread, still moist within its paper sack. He offered me two slices before handing me a couple of white pills and paper cup full of water. I would have eaten the whole loaf if he'd left it there with me, but he didn't. Maybe he thinks someone takes care of me when he's away. If that's the case, he thinks wrong.

Aunt Perdita hasn't bothered to check in on me, not even once. At least not when I'm awake. I would have known, too, because this house looks new and fancy but something within the walls groans, settling against the changes in temperature or the switchback of the breeze. Every noise sends my eyes to the door, expecting it to creak open slowly, revealing my grizzly fate. If a dude in a hockey mask holding a machete plans to sneak up on me, I hope he at least offers me a sandwich first.

Thinking about food makes my stomach rumble again and I sigh, knowing there's no other choice but to pull myself together and make the trek down to the kitchen. It's easier said than done. Besides my usual hobble, now a handful of purple bruises and a few broken ribs join the mix. Doc said I'd suffered another concussion, too, but he didn't seem real concerned about keeping me awake. What was it to anyone if I slipped away into a coma, never to be heard from again? It would make things easier for my aunt, I bet. Then she wouldn't be annoyed by the sight of me, and I wouldn't be blamed for sending away her precious hired help.

Millie wouldn't have let me go a day on only bread and water. The Millie I met would have cooked me one of everything in the kitchen, stuffing me until I couldn't hold another bite. Now that I think about it, I can't really blame Aunt Perdita for being upset that she's gone. *Oh, Millie. I barely met you, and I miss you, too.*

The walk down to the kitchen is more like an expedition. Each step shoots pain through me in a hundred frantic directions, and it's all I can do to keep from cursing as I make my way down the hall. I strain to look ahead of me as I shift my weight from my bad right hip to my tender left ankle, all while keeping an arm wrapped around my ribcage for protection. My free hand slides against the wall, ready to steady myself should one of my legs give out. *This is ridiculous. I should just let myself starve.*

When I finally reach the kitchen, I discover my efforts are in vain. The refrigerator houses one-quarter of a gallon of spoiled 2% milk, a package of grey bacon, a mushy kiwi fruit, and two bottles of salad dressing. In the cupboard, I unearth the heel from a loaf of wheat bread in an open plastic sack. Oh, and I can't forget about the box of stale corn flakes. Tears form in my eyes, and I collapse onto a stool next to the counter. Every fiber of my soul wants to throw things at my aunt for not taking care of me, for not being the kind of nurturing person her sister had been. Mom would have made sure I had food. She would have sat next to my bed and wiped my forehead with a cool cloth. She would have done anything and everything for me. I growl, the sound muffled by my hands as I bury my face in them. I don't know my aunt at all, but she's given me one more reason to hate her.

Obviously unable to scrape together anything safe enough to eat, I set off on the journey back to my room to change. Not that I care if anyone sees me in my dad's ratty Tigers t-shirt and cut-off sweats, but yoga pants and a long-sleeved shirt do a better job of hiding my new bruises. I'm an expert at hiding bruises. Even if no one else notices, masking my injuries is important to me. I don't want sympathy and I don't want anyone to fix me, because they can't fix what's truly broken.

With one more tug on the knot securing my periwinkle scarf, I pull open the front door and step outside into the day. A man in faded overalls hunches over a massive flowerbed on the other side of the drive. He's turned away from me, and I watch the muscles of his back flex beneath his red-and-white plaid shirt as he pulls weeds free from the soil. A thatched straw hat hides the top of his head so I can't immediately identify him, but I pray it's Oliver.

Stop it! I slam a wall down against my own thoughts. *He almost got me killed with his dumb, paranoid idea. There was nothing to be afraid of after all, unless you count his homicidal horse.*

There's nothing to be afraid of? Keep telling yourself that. Maybe you've forgotten, but I remember it all.

Shut up! I screech back. *I will not argue with myself. There's enough wrong with me! I'm not adding voices in my head to the list!*

Whatever. I saw what I saw. He saved you.

I told you, SHUT UP!

The man turns around. Though the brim of his hat shrouds his face in shadows, Norman's widened eyes still glow within their sockets. A trowel jitters in his trembling hand.

I make my way down the front steps, wincing the whole way. "Norman. That's your name, right?" I ask him, even though I know very well who he is. Even when he isn't *this close* to chopping off my head with a pair of garden shears, Norman strikes me as the kind of guy who makes an impression on people.

Norman stutters a step backward. His heels clip the first row of flowers, but he doesn't seem to notice.

I take another step. "I don't bite, promise."

My words don't put Norman at ease. If not for his shaking hands and the dip of his Adam's apple when he swallows, he appears petrified, frozen in place. Norman frightens me because of his overall size, all-around flightiness, and access to potential weapons. I must frighten him, too, because people disappear when I'm around.

Nonna's words echo back to me. "Lucy, they're more afraid of you than you are of them." She had been talking about bees at the time, but I pretend she'd meant startled black men like Norman, here. I bump up my smile another notch and take yet another step in his direction. His nostrils flare like a spooked horse—he's ready to bolt. Or attack. Or both. I clear my throat and Norman flinches.

"Look, I'm super hungry and I don't know if I can make it all the way into town for a bite to eat," I explain, wrapping my arms around myself. "Do you know of anyone around here who wouldn't mind making me a PB&J or something?"

He ignores my question. "Who—*what*—are you?" he demands. The whites of his eyes grow, and I wonder if it's possible for eyes to pop out like they do in the cartoons.

"Huh?" My smile falters. "I'm not a *what*. My name is Lucy." Feeling bold, I stick out my hand.

Norman retreats another step and crushes a pale yellow petunia plant under his work boot. "Don't you touch me, you hear? I don't want none of your trouble." His empty hand balls up at his side.

"Suit yourself," I say, pulling my hand back and then sidling out of his reach. His shoulders droop as I give him space. Still, he keeps his eyes on me until I step onto the street.

Oliver must have told Norman about Perdita's crazy niece and our argument over talking animals and lost scarves or whatever had finally pushed him away. I'm not the crazy one—at least, I don't think so—but everyone here trusts Oliver, including Norman. To the people of Mitte, I'm a threat.

I make it about three blocks before a cat darts between my feet and I crash to my hands and knees on the pavement. Gravel from the road beds into my palms and stings, but it's nothing compared to the lightning engulfing my chest. Gasping for air, I crumple onto my back in the middle of the empty street. I dare a car to run over me and finish the job. *Bring it on.*

A spotted face—the cat—bends over mine, studying me. She did this to me, clipping my already unsteady feet so I would fall. I don't know how I know this only by looking in her tawny eyes, but I know. Then she licks me on the nose with her sandpaper tongue; an apology. I ease myself up to sitting, biting the inside of my mouth at the jab of my crooked ribs. The cat slinks several paces away then sinks to her haunches. She watches me with expectation.

"Hi kitty-kitty," I say. "What do you want?"

The cat continues to stare.

"Do you want me to pet you?" I stretch my hand in her direction. She blinks in a show of feline indifference.

"Are you hungry, too?"

I'd made fun of Oliver for claiming to have conversations with his horse. Now here I am, sitting in the middle of the road, talking to a cat. Maybe I really have lost it.

My new friend yawns and arches her rear end to the sky, then pads off to my left. She winds her way around the mailbox post in front of one of the cookie-cutter houses on this block, then stops. When I don't respond, she reaches up the wooden post and drags her nails down. More rubbing up against the mailbox post. More blank stares from me. She's trying to convey some kind of message, but I suck at riddles and charades—especially with animals.

I scan our surroundings—houses, parked cars, cats, suburbia— and end up back at the mailbox. She meows and reaches up again to dig her claws into the post. Is she trying to tell me something about the mailbox? It's a mailbox, black plastic and ordinary, with the house number and name plastered on the side in metallic stickers. 5250 Orphanage.

Orphanage. Those still exist?

My eyes drift from the mailbox to the front of the house. My heart leaps when I notice a girl peering out at me from behind the cloudy picture window. So many of the scary movies I watched with Tanya included a pale orphan girl, usually possessed by a spirit bent on carrying out an unspeakably bloody plan. Ignoring my bones as they scream at me, I rocket to my feet, anxious to get away from evil wrapped up in the body of a precocious girl. My legs can only carry me so fast, but I push them to their limits. This body won't help my chances for survival against the kidpocalypse.

"Wait," a quiet voice chimes behind me. In a normal neighborhood, the buzz of a lawnmower or the stutter of a sprinkler might have drowned her out completely. But everything's too still.

I don't want to turn and move headlong into her trap, but I do anyway.

A girl who can't be more than six or seven stands on the sidewalk, in a pair of pink shorts and a plain white tank top that scrunches up a little bit around her belly. Her blonde hair frames the curve of her small face and eyes so blue they're almost fluorescent.

"I'm Magnolia," she offers, as if I'd asked.

"Hi, Magnolia." I search for an appropriate response while I decide if she's plotting to eat my soul or something. "That's a pretty name."

"Thank you. My momma . . ." She looks at her bare feet, and I think I catch the wobble of her lower lip.

"Well, it's lovely," I say. Thinking about my momma makes me feel sad, too, so I change the subject fast. "My name's Lucy. Can I help you with something?"

Magnolia brings her gaze back to mine and shakes her head, her hair swinging like the boughs of a willow in a storm. "No, ma'am. But I can help you." She smiles, revealing a wide gap of missing teeth in the front of her mouth.

Could soul-snatchers be this adorable?

I soften. "Oh yeah? How can you help me?"

The girl points a stubby finger toward the calico cat, now nestled in the crook of an old oak tree. "Patches told me you got hurt real bad and you ain't got no food to eat."

Patches regards me from her perch and blinks.

A talking cat, of course.

Though goosebumps travel along my forearms and the back of my neck, I nod. "Patches is a smart cat."

"We got a lot of food in the kitchen. Miss Letty cooks real good."

Before I can say no, Magnolia laces her fingers with mine. She leads me up the walk to the stoop and pulls open the pocked screen door.

"Miss Letty won't mind you bringing a stranger in the house?" I raise my eyebrow.

The girl giggles. It reminds me of a chorus of baby birds. "You're silly, Lucy. You're not a stranger. You lost your momma and daddy just like us. I bet Miss Letty would let you stay, if you wanted."

My mouth drops open. *I'm an orphan.* In a strange way, that makes the kids within these walls my kin. I stop resisting her pull and enter the house.

Chapter 8

"Oh," says the woman at the sink. Soapsuds cling to her fingers as she rests a hand on her heart. "You've brought company, Maggie?"

"Yu-huh!" With curls bobbing, Maggie drags me over to a long table with benches that reminds me a lot of a picnic table, except I've never see anyone with a picnic table in their kitchen. "This is Lucy. Lucy ain't got no family. Can she stay?"

From Letty's open mouth, I can tell she's been put on the spot. I blush at the child's forwardness and shake my head. "Oh, no. It's okay. I'm staying with my aunt just down the road."

Letty's thin shoulders relax as she returns to the dishes. "You're Perdita's niece, I take it?"

"Yeah." The woman's rod-straight spine stiffens even further at my flippant reply. Anxious not to land on Letty's bad side right off the bat, I correct myself. "Yes, ma'am. I'm Lucy Torres." I cringe when I say my last name. I'm the last living Torres, a shivering leaf clinging to my withered family tree. The weight of my situation settles on my shoulders.

Letty watches me for a moment before drying her hands on a towel tucked in the waistband of her apron. With a flutter of her fingertips, she shoos Magnolia away. "Go on, child. I do believe you forgot to tidy your bed. There'll be no playing with your new friend until you do."

Magnolia sticks out her lower lip in a pout, but runs off to do as the woman instructs. I watch her until she disappears around the corner. Once we're alone, Letty turns her attention to me.

"Perdita isn't well, as you probably know."

I nod.

"I worry about anyone who spends too much time around that woman, but that's neither here nor there." Letty pauses and strokes the long silver braid cascading down her shoulder. Her eyes are the color of steel wool and they scrub away at me until I squirm beneath my skin. Finally, she says, "Can I trust you, Lucy?"

I blink a few times at the question. "Yeah, I think so."

"What I do here is very important to me. I cannot risk harming my little ones beyond what harm has already come to them. If I cannot trust you, I need you to go."

"You can trust me," I vow, and I mean it.

"Good. Then that's settled." She grins. The lines accentuating her mouth suggest she used to be happy a lot. "You're welcome here, Lucy, if you need a break from Perdita, and I reckon you will. Of course, you can't be here after dark, but that goes without saying."

I want to ask her why it goes without saying, why no one is allowed to do anything after dark, but I bob my head instead.

She pats my hand and stands. "You look absolutely peaked. Maggie was right to ask you in."

I offer her a weak smile. "Aunt Perdita isn't the best at stocking the kitchen. I think she's too used to having Millie around."

"When's the last time you've eaten?"

"Sometime yesterday. Doc brought me some bread to help settle my stomach so I could take my meds."

Letty's eyes narrow. "Medication? What for, if you don't mind me askin'?"

Truth is, I do mind, but the idea of refusing Letty anything frightens me a little. She's the kind of old lady who wouldn't hesitate to tan your hide with a switch if she thought you needed it. "It's nothing. I fell down the other day."

Magnolia chooses that moment to run back into the room. "Patches told me Oliver's horse fell over, right on top of her," she says matter-of-factly as she plunks herself back down on the bench.

The old woman glares back at me, crossing her arms. "Nothing, eh?"

A flush creeps across my face at being caught in my half-truth. It's been a while since I've had to answer to anyone. "Technically, the horse didn't fall on me. Oliver fell on me. We were . . ." What *were* we doing? I don't even know. We had been running from something, but I couldn't remember what.

"Be thankful it was only a few bumps and bruises, then. If they'd caught you, it would have been so much worse." Momentarily satisfied by my confession, Letty breaks her iron gaze to move toward the refrigerator. "Now, how does a cold chicken sandwich sound?

I spend the rest of the afternoon hanging out with the other children at the orphanage. There are three in all: the oldest a fourteen-year-old boy named Duke; another girl, Tessa; and Magnolia. They all want to hear about growing up in Detroit, and I tell them story after story until Letty calls us to set up for dinner.

It's the first time since the accident that I feel comfortable. It's the first time in a long time that

I've actually had a conversation without getting angry. When one of my stories leaves me choked up, the kids don't press me to talk about it. They know how it feels. Their hearts are full of sad stories, too.

Too soon, the sun sinks toward the horizon. It's time for me to go home, the last place I want to be.

I slip into the mansion a few minutes before sunset, tired and aching from too much walking on my twisted frame. The halls echo with my stumbling steps, which I'm sure really annoys Aunt Perdita. Well, she really annoys me, too, so I stomp more loudly than necessary. Just to get under her skin.

When I flip on the light in my room, a new rose floats in the crystal vase next to my bed.

Chapter 9

I'd just finished lacing up my sneakers when the knock on the door startles me.

"Come in," I say. Aunt Perdita must really be bored to wander all the way to my room. I hadn't seen her in days. She's the worst guardian ever.

The door opens and Oliver, not my aunt, stands in the doorway. He nervously shifts his weight from side to side.

"Turn around! I'm not decent!" I shield my bald head with my hands. I don't care if my aunt sees me at my worst; her opinion doesn't matter to me one bit. Wish I could say the same for Oliver.

He whirls away from me, clearing his throat. "I'm real sorry. I should have sent your aunt."

I grab the first scarf I find dangling from the post of my bed and work at wrapping it around to hide the worst of my scars. "Relax," I say. "I'm not naked or anything. You can look now."

When he turns around, his face is red. A laugh sputters from my lips.

"Luce, I only came here to give you this." He pulls my lost scarf from his pocket. "There's not much left of it, but I told you I'd find it. I like to keep my word."

That scarf had been one of my favorites, a faint lilac with silver threads woven in a series of spirals. My best-tolerated nurse, Greta, had given it to me on her last shift before my discharge. Now it barely resembles the same item, one end shredded and singed beyond recognition. I hug the fabric to my chest and frown. "What in the world happened to it?"

Oliver opens his mouth to answer, but seems to think better of it.

I place the tattered remains of my scarf on the table next to the rose vase. "Well, thanks for returning it, I guess."

He doesn't move.

"If that's all, I've got to go. The kids begged Letty to let me take them to the fountain. And Maggie wants ice cream."

"Downtown?" His voice drops. "I don't think that's such a good idea. I've heard some of the—"

Irritation bubbles within me. "I won't be alone. Don't worry, *Dad*." I instantly regret my words. Even on his very best day, Oliver will never come close to being as awesome as my father had been. He had one thing right, though—my dad would have worried about me alone in a place like this, too. I sigh and close my eyes. "Sorry . . . I didn't mean that."

Oliver looks away, but concern shines clearly in his dark eyes. "Those kids can't do a thing to protect you if you need it. Letty hasn't thought this through."

"What kind of town is this? I'm not even safe in the center of Main Street in broad daylight?"

His face remains sober. "So you see my point."

"Not really."

He narrows the gap between us, our faces so close together our noses nearly touch. Threads of green braid into the brown of his irises, eyes the color of earth itself. For one suspended moment, I expect him to lean in for a kiss. My palms grow sticky and my throat won't cooperate when I try to swallow.

He's going to kiss me! I'm so not ready for this. My last kiss ruined my life.

I brace for impact, squeezing my eyes shut. Instead of a kiss, Oliver grasps my shoulders in each of his hands, wrestling my attention away from Derek Carver and his trash-talking mouth.

"Luce, Mitte isn't like anywhere you've ever been before," he says. His eyes flash like lightning striking the earth. "The rules don't apply here. I keep trying to tell you."

I shrug away from his grip. I'm trapped under his warning and I need to free myself. "Help me out, then. It's like I'm in the Twilight Zone!"

Oliver remains quiet.

"I swear—I'm going to go insane if I can't go anywhere or do anything. Can't you tell me anything?" My last sentence isn't a question. It's a plea.

Thoughts war in the shift of his eyes, the twitch of his lips, the tightening of his jaw. He wants to share everything with me, I can tell. But when he opens his mouth to speak, it snaps back closed.

I can't stand it anymore.

"If you're not going to say anything, then I guess I'll go. Ignorance is bliss and junk." I limp away, missing my ability to stalk out like an angry lioness. Stupid bionic leg. So much for fixing me up like new. I can't even make a dramatic exit anymore.

My retreat is so slow that Oliver could take his time making a list of the pros and cons of telling me all about Mitte. Heck, my retreat is so slow he could work a crossword puzzle, knit a sweater, and then make his list. I only make it a few doors down before he speaks up.

"If you're not going to take my word for it, then all I can do is wish you luck."

I roll my eyes as I continue my slow progress down the hall.

"But if you're still around later, maybe we could talk."

"Okay," I sigh, tired of the mystery. "I'll be back eventually."

We reach the front door together, which he swings outward with a flair. "Well, then, 'eventually' it is, ma'am. I hope."

"Still not a ma'am!" I call out as I walk away.

The kids' voices begin buzzing as soon as we near the shops on the fringe of downtown Mitte. Magnolia, who had just peeled her face from the window of the bakery, The Baking Mitte, looks practically combustible.

"Oh, thankyouthankyouthankyou for bringing us, Lucy!" she trills as she spins in a circle and knocks into Tessa. Remembering her manners, Magnolia straightens the hem of her tank top and says, "Oops. Sorry, Tess."

Tessa wrinkles her nose, driving her freckles together in a blob. She is ten years old, with stick-straight red hair, and has never spoken a word in the time I've been around her. Magnolia ignores her rebuttal and skips back to my side. "Can we get cookies on the way home? Miss Letty doesn't let us have them."

"I don't know, Mags. Cookies and ice cream in one day? Letty might not let me take you anywhere ever again." I laugh. "Besides, you've already got too much energy. I can't keep up."

"Too bad you can't drive, Lucy," Duke says. "You're slow."

"Hey!" I punch his arm. "I can drive better than you." It's not true. My driving is abysmal and the reason I'm stuck in Mitte. But Duke doesn't know that.

A grin creeps across his face. "You know how to drive?"

"Yeah, but I . . . don't drive." My smile disappears as the truck's horn blares in my mind. "Long story. But maybe I can teach you someday." The words feel like a lie as soon as they trip off my lips. I'm not sure how I'll ever get behind the wheel of another vehicle, not when I can still hear them dying in my memories.

"Oh. Yeah, that's not gonna happen," Duke mutters, shoving his hands into the pockets of his worn jeans.

I nudge his shoulder with mine. "Why not? Afraid a girl's a better driver than you?"

He purses his lips and puts a step between us.

"Ladies and gentlemen!" I cup my hands around my mouth to make my voice louder. "Duke is intimidated by my mad skills!" Mad skills are an extreme exaggeration, but no one in Mitte knows about the accident. Never would, if I could help it.

"Am not," he says. A fringe of ink-black bangs hides his eyes. "But you know they won't let us drive, even if I was old enough."

"Who won't?" All I can picture is a room full of pruney town council members taking a vote on whether residents of Mitte were permitted to drive cars. The council members would unanimously agree that, no, cars were evil. Then they would jot that rule down next to the "no dogs" and the "no going outside after dark" rules.

"You're kidding, right?" Duke scrunches up his face like I've sprouted a second head. Apparently I should already know the answer to my question. And, of course, he knows the answer. Everyone knows everything about this place except for me—so what else is new?

I sigh.

His lip curls into a sneer. "The Conductors would have our skin if we so much as touched the cars, you know that."

"The Conductors?"

He snorts. "How hard did you hit your head?"

I smile but I have no idea what he's talking about or, worse yet, *who* he's talking about. Most of my time in this town I've spent alone, trapped in the house by a lack of sunlight or stupid broken bones. It's difficult to learn the rules that way.

Someone really ought to have given me the Mitte Handbook or something.

Ask him.

The thought flickers in my head only long enough for me to squash it flat like a bug. Duke thinks I know what I'm doing and, worse than that, he might even look up to me. I might even *matter* to him. I shake my head. No. I stopped mattering months ago when I became a broken thing in need of mending instead of a seventeen-year-old girl with dreams of her own.

Ask him. It might save you.

I bite my tongue and push the voice back into the furthest corner of my head. Of course I can't ask him to give me Mitte 101, and why do I need to? Mitte's just a close-minded, crazy little town identical to a thousand others. It's the kind of town country songs whine about, the kind of town that suffocates kids like me until they find refuge in the big city—any big city, take your pick.

My smile widens into a devious grin. I nudge him again with my elbow, pushing him off balance. "C'mon. What they don't know won't hurt 'em."

Duke's eyes widen beneath their cover. "Someone would tell on us, Luce. You know they would. This place is bad enough." He pauses and a tremor shakes his frame. "I can't imagine being sent away, and I don't want to."

My insides scream at me to pull him aside and ask him exactly what he means by that, but my pride keeps my mouth shut. Being sent away sounds like a pretty good option to me, but Duke's reaction convinces me to tuck away any thoughts of escape. For now.

The babbling voices of the fountain trickle down the street, interrupting a daydream in which I was running up the front steps of my old house and into my dad's open arms. I push the lump in my throat down with a swallow, forcing myself to concentrate on the younger children, who are in the process of running into traffic.

Traffic. I snort. *You mean scary-looking Angus sitting on the bench, cracking his knuckles through his gloves? The withered old lady shuffling down the center of the street in her threadbare housecoat? As long as no one breaks a hip here, I think we're good.*

I follow Magnolia's golden head as it bounces away in the distance. Thankfully she opts for the safest path of several choices, the sidewalk across the street from the burly motorcyclist now giving me the evil eye. At least, I'm pretty sure he's giving me the evil eye. No one else seems to notice his hostility—or maybe he's always like this and they've grown used to it. I ignore Angus' flesh-eating glare but speed up my hobble . . . just in case.

"Girl!" he barks.

Hop-step. Hop-step. Hop-step.

"Hey, you!" He tries again.

Hop-step. Hop-step. Hop-

"Quit runnin' or whatever you wanna call that, *freak!*"

Step.

The tips of my ears heat up. I can't argue my freakishness with Angus; I know he's more right than wrong. Does he really have to say it out loud, though? Maybe someone within earshot hasn't figured it out yet and he totally just clued them in.

Thanks a lot, jerk.

And it's not like he has room to talk. At least I'm not the one dressed head-to-toe in black leather on an 80-degree day.

Not willing to give him more than a glance over my shoulder, I pull my mouth into a tight line. "What is it? I'm kind of in a hurry." The kids, minus Duke, are still on the move toward the fountain.

Angus strides up to me in a handful of jingling steps. Even though he sports a beer belly and his leather pants appear to be cutting off the circulation to the lower half of his body, his agility still trumps mine. I shrink back a step. I'd back up more than that, but Duke moves forward and braces himself at my right shoulder.

"Angus, she's not a freak. You apologize to her right now," Duke says through gritted teeth.

My eyes flit toward Duke in surprise, but I don't dare take my focus from the biker. The man chuckles and curls his fingers into a fist, the leather of his gloves creaking.

I reach back for Duke, and when I connect with his hand, I squeeze. Hard. "It's okay," I say, forcing the corners of my mouth upward even though smiling's the last thing I want to do. Duke's fingers tremble in mine for a moment then reluctantly return my squeeze.

Angus' beady eyes narrow, not missing the communication between us. "Cut that out," he spits, motioning wildly at our entwined hands. "I know what you're doing."

Truth is, I don't even know what I'm doing. Maybe Angus can fill me in.

Ask him, I dare you.

A small crowd has formed around us, attracted like moths to a flame by the boom of Angus' words. Some of the faces I recognize from the diner. Some are strangers. Each of them wears different shades of similar expressions, ranging from suspicion to flat-out hatred. The little old lady previously wandering down the street oscillates between pity and confusion. Sal, the burly Italian from the diner, towers over everyone. His upper lip curls over his teeth in a sneer that shoots ice through my veins.

"I—I don't know what you're—" My palm turns clammy in Duke's grasp.

Duke, still holding on tight, places himself between me and most of the angry throng. "Leave her alone." His voice is steady, but his pulse races against my skin.

"Duke," I murmur. "It's okay. I can handle this."

My words don't put him at ease.

"I'm taking the kids to see the fountain, that's all," I say, even though I don't owe them an explanation.

"Over my dead body. You ain't takin' those kids nowhere," Angus snarls, lunging forward. Several in the crowd chuckle, an unexpected response to his threat, and I skim the crowd trying to figure out what's so funny. Taking my eyes off the boulder of a man advancing on me is a big mistake.

Duke hadn't been thrown off, though, and he shields me from the brunt of the attack. They both grunt as they collide and fall to the concrete with a sickening thud. No one moves, frozen in horror at Angus on top of the young boy, his gloved fist drawn back like a cobra ready to strike.

Trapped beneath Angus' legs, Duke lies still, his eyes rolled back in his head.

Chapter 10

I don't know how long I scream before the townspeople turn from broken Duke back to me. Any waver of kindness they'd felt before is long gone. Their piercing eyes blame me for what happened to Duke. I blame me, too.

"Duke? Duke!" I crumple next to his limp body. "Can you hear me?" Tears spill from my eyes as I bury my face in the tuft of hair sticking out above his ear. "I'm so sorry. I never meant for this to happen."

The boy doesn't stir.

Someone else I cared for is dead. I'm cursed, I can see that now. Swallowing hard, I raise myself up until Angus and I are nearly eye-to-eye.

"You all can do with me what you want. I don't want to live anymore if all I do is hurt people." My lip quivers, betraying my resolve, but I'm on their side. My existence ended Duke's life. Whatever fate these people have planned for me can't undo that, but at least it will keep it from happening again.

Angus jeers, but I'm not afraid of him anymore. I'm not afraid of anyone or anything anymore. I'm numb.

I run my thumb over the smooth skin of Duke's cheek, trying to memorize the peacefulness of his face before I leave him.

"Sal," Angus grunts. With some difficulty and a great deal of squeaking leather, he hoists himself up from the boy's frail body, "the girl's surrendering. Get the—"

Before he can finish, a great clattering crescendos from an alley to my back.

"Lucy!"

This time I recognize Oliver's voice before I see him. I struggle to stand, whirling just in time for Oliver to gallop by on Jasper. With a free arm, he hooks me around my waist and sweeps me from the sidewalk. It looks so easy when they do it in the movies. In real life, it's terrifying, and I almost black out from the stab of my disjointed ribs. As I dangle under Oliver's arm, Jasper's hind legs tangle with mine. Fueled by a surge of adrenaline, I claw my way onto his back, behind Oliver.

When I finally feel secure—or as secure as I'm going to get—I risk a glance back to the people gathered around Duke's body on the street. Frustration twists their faces, but not Sal and Angus. They look like they would rip me apart with their bare hands if given the chance. Even though I want to be free of this life, relief floods over me as we distance ourselves from the crowd.

I lean forward to shout in his ear, "What in the heck are you doing?"

"What does it look like I'm doing?" Oliver urges Jasper forward with his heels. "I'm being the knight in shining armor."

"You saved the wrong person," I say so quietly I'm sure Jasper's hoofbeats cover my words.

"No, I didn't."

How can Oliver suggest my life means more than Duke's? My life is nothing—less than nothing. Duke, at least, had never felt the pain of watching his family die at his own hands. He hadn't needed a second chance at life because he'd still been doing okay with his first.

Even though I'm upset with Oliver for rescuing me instead, I wrap my arms tighter around his middle and hide my face against his shoulder. My tears soak into the coarse threads of Oliver's linen shirt, the circle of moisture growing with each drop. He won't care; if I needed it, he would take the shirt off his back and let me use it as a handkerchief—that's the kind of guy he is. He's nothing like me.

"How could you be so selfish?" Unspoken pain fills Mom's eyes.

I swing the car around the corner faster than I should have, and Dad has to brace himself against the side of the car to keep from falling over. "How could I be so selfish?" I ask, unsure I'd heard her correctly. "That's all you can say? Real nice, Mom."

The sooner we eat dinner and get back home, the better, because I don't think I can sit in this car one second longer than necessary. Not with all their judgment and—grrrrr!

The light far ahead of us shines green, and I breathe a 'thank you' to God for shaving some time off our commute. Pressing my foot down on the gas pedal, we race toward the intersection.

Jasper slows to a walk once Oliver figures we're out of immediate danger. It's quiet here, wherever we are, except for the rhythmic groan of Jasper's saddle with each step. When I lift my head from Oliver's shirt, the forest crowds in around us. The low boughs of the trees shield us from sight and muffle our movements with a carpet of dried pine needles. A short way off to our right, a flat ribbon of cement stretches endlessly in both directions.

I'm anxious someone driving by will discover us, but I shouldn't be. Not one vehicle passes us.

The air is silent. Waiting. It seems foolish to speak, to confirm our location to anyone tracking us, so I lean forward until my lips almost brush Oliver's earlobes. "Where are we going?" I whisper.

Oliver pauses and glances over his shoulder at me before he answers. It's like he's taking a picture, preserving this moment in his mind because . . . because why? A shift of the wind fans the hair from his eyes as I search them for the answer. His ghost of a smile fails to disguise the sadness I find there.

Why does this feel like good-bye? I hate this place, but I hate the thought of Oliver dumping me in the middle of the forest like a wild animal even more.

"You wanted to talk, so we're going to talk," he says finally, straightening up and turning his attention to our path.

"It's about time, just sayin'."

"Yeah, well, if you want a prayer of surviving here, I guess I don't have much of a choice, do I? It's not like I can guard you twenty-four-seven." Oliver rubs his forehead with his palm. Clearly, I'm a pain in the butt. That's something we have in common.

"So go right ahead. I'm listening."

"Relax, Lucy. We're almost there."

Everything around us appears the same as it had a mile back, and the mile before that. The same evergreens with prickles running up and down their spines. The same expanse of silver pavement, vacant and still. The same whistle of wind playing a soft duet to the horse's footfalls. We could have been walking in circles, for all I know.

Beneath me, Jasper's muscles begin to shiver. His easy, flowing gait shortens until he feels coiled up like a spring ready to bound off. Without warning, the gelding shies sideways, snaking his head around in the direction we'd come. Though my arms still encircle Oliver's middle, my seat slides sideways at the swift change of direction. For one awful second our eyes meet, mine and Jasper's, and his terror reflects back to me. I know that look too well, except the last time I experienced it, I'd been staring down death disguised as an 18-wheeler.

"Easy, boy." Oliver places a reassuring hand on the horse's trembling shoulder.

"Oliver!" I cry, clawing at his stomach to keep my balance. "I'm falling!"

With some effort, Oliver pries loose from my grip and swings his left leg over the front of his saddle. Freeing himself from Jasper, he drops to his feet, cushioned by the spongy earth. Jasper's head flies upward, startled, until he realizes his only remaining rider—me—has zero control over the situation. He flattens his neck out and accelerates like he's just cleared the starting gate of the Kentucky Derby.

I topple sideways off Jasper as he shoots forward in blind panic. Big surprise there. Next would come the impact, the sickening crunch of more of my bones against the ground. Maybe this time I wouldn't break anything, but that's not my kind of luck. My body has been disintegrating into increasingly smaller pieces ever since the wreck. I've become brittle and delicate, always one wrong step away from crumbling into a pile of unrecognizable rubble.

Head-first, I hurtle towards the soil. There's no time to fear what will happen to my brain when the scaffolding holding the mosaic of my skull together gives way. I'm not afraid to die, to blink and then pass from this life to whatever happens next. My parents wait for me there, ready to scoop me into their arms, our family complete once more. I close my eyes and smile, welcoming the end.

Of course, Oliver catches me. Cradled in his arms, his heart thunders against my cheek. I force myself to swallow, to push down the annoying rush of relief at his rescue and the swirl in my stomach stirred up by his embrace. I don't want to be here. No matter how my own flesh tries to argue against my feelings, I am ticked off to still be alive. As soon as he rests my toes on the ground and lets me go, I haul back with my best right hook and catch him in the nose.

"What the—" he cries, clasping his hands to his face. A trickle of crimson runs through his fingers and seeps into the cuff of his linen shirt. His hands hide most of his face, but the hurt in his dark eyes is unmistakable. "What'd you do that for?"

I don't answer. Instead, I spin on my heel and stalk off in the opposite direction from Oliver, Jasper, and Mitte. There's nothing else around but trees stretching as far as I can see. The breeze presses against me and slows my angry progress.

All this time, the fragrance of the forest had been damp and tangy. But now there's something else, something sharp and sulfuric. Smoke. Someone lives out here, or maybe a wildfire blazes in the distance. Either I can find shelter with this stranger in the woods, or I'll burn to ashes curled against the charred trunk of a pine. It doesn't matter anymore. Fueled by my lame new plan, I forge into the twisted overgrowth of vines ahead.

"Stop," Oliver says, closer to me than I expect.

I want to punch him again for following me. I want to punch him just to punch *something* because my lack of speed frustrates me. Before everything fell apart, I'd have left him in a cloud of dust, putting miles between us before my heart had a chance to react. Running effortlessly, another thing I'd lost to the crash. I turn to spit in Oliver's general vicinity, but I continue limping forward.

"Lucy, you've got to listen to me." He grasps my elbow from behind. "Stop, *now*."

I wrench free from his grip. "Let go of me." The words hiss through my teeth. "You're just as crazy as the rest of them, you know that?"

"If you keep walking, I can't save you from what happens next."

"Good. Don't bother." My bitter laugh rings through the small distance between us. I want him to give up, to make this easy on both of us.

When he shuffles one more step behind me, I whirl around with my hands balled at my side. "Why won't you leave me alone?" I say.

"Your name—Lucille—" My eyes narrow when he uses my full name. "It means 'light.'"

I cross my arms, annoyed by his sudden need for pointless trivia. "So?"

"So . . . I've been waiting for you for a long time."

I snort. "Quit being so creepy, Oliver."

"I promise I'm not trying to scare you. But you're different from the others."

My eyes roll toward the canopy of feathery boughs overhead. Pick-up lines at a time like this? "I'm different? Give me one reason why I'm so special because, personally, I think you're full of it."

He runs a hand through his dark hair, choosing his words carefully.

"Forget I asked," I sigh. Desperate to put space between us, I hobble in the direction Oliver doesn't want me to go. Tension vibrates in the air between us, but I don't care anymore.

"Wait," he cries, his voice desperate. "You're not like anyone else . . . because you're not dead."

Chapter 11

A wall slams down inside my brain, shielding me from the full impact of Oliver's words.

"Lucy, say something. Please?"

I can't answer him, and, after his revelation, I sure can't trust him. Conversation is definitely out, as is hanging around him for one second more. I'd made a big mistake by feeling anything for anyone in this town—Duke, Magnolia, Oliver, *anyone*. I set my jaw and wrap myself in numbness. *It won't happen again.*

All I want is distance and silence. My only option, then, is to put one foot in front of the other and stumble into the blanket of smoke. I pray Oliver will finally get the hint and stay away. And he does. Before I can decide whether or not that makes me happy, a spark shoots down my spine.

Random aches and pains are the norm for me, so I shrug it off.

Being slow as a turtle—even slower than that, sometimes—isn't my norm. My body's built to be aerodynamic, thin and sleek. I used to be as light and graceful as a gazelle, my legs bounding me forward with ease. They said I would go places, that I'd have my pick of colleges. Coach lined up recruiters for our biggest meets, and all I had to do was show up and let go. My heart would do the rest.

I miss the wind in my face and the teardrops collecting in the corners of my eyes as everything blurred behind me. I miss the crunch of pebbles beneath my shoes. I miss the tickle of my ponytail grazing the back of my neck with each swaying step. I miss pushing through the burn in my lungs and deep within my legs. *Faster, faster, faster.* I miss every single shin splint and weeping blister. I miss running so hard the world spins behind my eyes, struggling to catch up. Heck, I even miss throwing up in the grass because I pushed myself to my limit. Even the worst day on the track pales in comparison to my life now. This isn't life.

They said I would go places. Somehow, I doubt this is what they meant.

I bite my lip to keep from sobbing as I creep forward. The forest falls silent around me except for the crackle of pine needles under my feet. The air grows so thick and heavy it presses on my chest, forcing me to stop to draw in a deep breath. My throat burns with the effort, and I cough. The fire is near, and so is my rescue.

Ahead, the pines crowd closer together, branches intertwined in protest. Even the forest wants to keep me prisoner. If I want to find an opening large enough to squeeze through, I'll have to follow this wall of green to the left or right instead of continuing straight ahead. Sideways frustrates me. Sideways won't get me away from Oliver or Mitte, the two things I want to be free of more than anything.

It's not one of my brightest ideas, but I grit my teeth and push forward into the arms of the pines. The needles welcome me, sliding across my skin like feathers. The tang of pine tar overpowers the smell of soot and destruction. Spreading apart the tangled branches in front of me, I smile. This isn't so bad, after all. This plan just might work.

But before I can shoot an *Adios, Oliver!* over my shoulder, the forest turns against me. Needles prick my lips and tiny beads of blood pop up wherever they make contact with my skin. I yelp as I try to bring my arms up to shield my face, which only makes me more of a human pincushion. No one comes to help me, even though it's pretty obvious I'm in trouble.

That means Oliver left. He *left*.

Not even two minutes ago, I had wanted as far away from that boy as humanly possible. Finally something had gone my way, and I can't even enjoy it. From where I cower, being mauled by flesh-eating vegetation, I curse Oliver for actually listening to me.

If Dad was here, he'd have torn himself in two to protect me. There's no way he would have let me wander off alone into the wilderness, no matter how much I kicked and screamed. Dad would have kicked and screamed right back at me, and then, when he'd had enough, he would have thrown me over his shoulder and carried me back to safety. I would have hated him every step of the way, as much as I loved him. He knew never to give up on me, but it doesn't matter anymore. Even Dad has abandoned me.

A flood of anger surges through me, and its intensity vibrates wildly across my skin like a bolt of lightning. Feeling sorry for myself won't do a single thing except kill me faster. I'm no damsel in distress, and this is the furthest thing from a fairy tale. Death will track me to this forest, one way or another. A man can't stop the inevitable; I feel it as sure as the pulse pounding in my veins. Wiping the blood from my mouth, I force myself further into the green.

Goosebumps spring up on the back of my neck and ripple down my arms. *What in the—?* The frantic rhythm of my heart slamming through my body crushes the breath from my lungs.

My Papa suffered his first heart attack right in front of me as I blew out the candles on my birthday cake on my tenth birthday. I'll never forget—his eyes bugged out of his head like a fish out of water, gulping for air and finding none. The pressure building up in my chest makes me think of Papa. Will someone come across my body curled at the base of these trees, my eyes wide with fear like my grandfather? My body shudders at the thought.

No, my body just shudders. Everything around me shudders, too. Far below the blanket of scorched pine needles, the earth rolls as if a herd of stampeding buffalo will plow through the brush and trample me at any moment. There's something so familiar about all of this, but my mind can't connect the pieces.

The rumbling grows louder, like a freight train set on a collision course with my grove of trees. My brain can't focus on anything, but I know I need to move, and I need to move now. But in what direction? I turn my head from right to left and back again, but all I can see are the pine trees enveloping me.

An oppressive breeze shivers through the boughs, sending a branch skittering across the back of my neck. The way the heat prickles the skin of my back and then shrinks away almost convinces me that the Devil himself has trapped me in this place.

Hot. Nothing. Hot. Nothing.

The stench of death and decay assaults my nostrils, replacing the organic aroma of sap and soot. It smells like I'd stumbled across particularly hideous roadkill left to fester and bloat in the summer sun. I'm afraid to move and set off a chain reaction of horror movie proportions, but I risk looking at my feet. What if I hadn't stepped in woodland gore, but something else?

Hot. Nothing. Hot. Nothing.

I freeze in place, holding my breath as if my stillness will somehow protect me. Breathing or not, I know it doesn't matter. I am being hunted.

My hands tremble and I can't stand it anymore. If I'm going to die, I'm going to do it staring my predator right in the face, not with my back turned. Eyes wide, I whirl around, a branch slicing deep into my thigh in the process. A wayward sprig of pine finds its way into my open mouth when I cry out, and I sputter to spit it out.

Nothing's there. It was just me being paranoid.

My shoulders droop as I release a weak laugh. Back to Plan A, getting the heck out of Mitte.

When I turn around, I'm staring straight into the face of . . .

What stands before me is indescribable—a mass of flames and smoke walking upright on legs like a man. It studies me like a viper trained in on a mouse about to become snake food. I'm not sure this creature has lips, but its tongue slides across where its lips should be, revealing several awful rows of charred teeth. A long streamer of saliva drips from its mouth, landing on my tank top.

"What have we here?" it rasps, stroking my jawline with one of its fiery claws. My skin blisters beneath its touch, and I bite back tears. The creature nods its head to my right, to someone or something I can't see. "This one is different. Methinks transportation is the only solution. What say you?"

There are more of them? The thought makes bile swim in my mouth.

Another voice. "Master's orders are clear: any who dare to cross the boundary must be transported."

Transportation. Clearly they aren't talking about heading downtown on the bus. My vision blurs, and I sway on my feet.

"Aye!" the thing barks, clasping my wrist in its grip. Beneath its fierce touch, my skin sizzles and blackens. My legs buckle as the curtain lowers on my tragic life.

Chapter 12

I'm moving. Someone's carrying me, but I don't want to open my eyes to find out who it is. The unspeakable, impossible thing I'd just seen—the abomination that had sized me up for its next meal—could be dragging me back to its pit for proper seasoning. The less I see, the less I think about it at all, the better. I shut my mind down, forcing myself to think of nothing.

Before I completely tuck myself away into stand-by mode, something rubs my cheek. Fabric, coarse against the raw skin on my jaw. I flinch at the contact, but it does not burn. Relief washes over me and I allow the tiniest of exhales, hoping my captor won't notice.

The reek of decay has disappeared. In its place is the perfume of the forest and something else I can't put my finger on, something sweet. None of this makes sense. The monster all up in my face not too long ago definitely lacked a great deal in the hygiene department. Plus, it hadn't been wearing a stitch of clothing.

I let my eyelids part enough to make out my captor's broad chest, covered in a rumpled linen shirt and suspenders.

No way. No. Freaking. Way.

"Thank heavens you're awake, Lucy." Oliver sighs. Beads of perspiration line his forehead even though he isn't struggling much under my weight. "I really thought I'd lost you back there."

When I try to speak, my throat won't cooperate. It feels like I've gargled a cup full of razors. Finally, I croak, "How . . . ?"

He shakes his head, his chocolate eyes fixed ahead of us. "Now's not the time. I can't take the risk they'll change their mind."

I'm not sure what he means, but I don't press him with my questions. He saved me again, even though he had every right to leave me to die. There, in his arms, I promise myself I won't fight against him anymore, and I won't risk either of our lives again. At least, not today.

Ignoring the sting from my ruined skin, I rest my head against his chest instead. "Thank you," I breathe into his shoulder.

"You would have done the same for me."

I don't share Oliver's confidence in me. That fire person was, no doubt about it, the most horrific thing I'd ever encountered. Face-to-ghoulish face again, I wouldn't hesitate to throw just about anyone else into its claws if it meant saving myself. If that makes me a bad person, then I'm guilty as charged.

Eventually we come to a log cabin hidden under the wings of a strand of evergreens. Jasper grazes near the edge of the cabin's porch, where the grass has grown tall enough to brush the floorboards. He raises his head in greeting as we approach, then goes back to nibbling. As happy as I am not to be some demon's dinner, I am *not* thrilled to see that horse again. I scowl in his direction, and Jasper snorts in reply. The feeling is, clearly, mutual.

"Now, I wouldn't be too rough on ol' Jasper." Oliver grins. "Truth be told, he did what we should have done from the start. We had no business being anywhere near The Divide."

"The what?"

Oliver eases me to my feet before replying. "The Divide."

"Should that mean something to me? You're forgetting that no one has bothered to tell me a thing about this place. Still." I take a step forward and stumble, catching my balance by grabbing his arm. Pain shoots through my wrist, and then I remember the creature's caustic grasp on my arm.

Oliver's eyebrows furrow as he steadies me. "Are you okay? You should sit down."

"I'm fine," I snap, then rub my face with my hands. "Sorry. I just really, really want to know more. About this Divide-thingy."

Oliver scans the flickering shadows around the cabin before answering. His voice is a low hum and I have to lean in to hear him. "The 'Divide-thingy' is what you were trying to walk through. We're not allowed there. That's why they came for you."

"What in the world was that thing, Oliver?"

Instead of answering me, he places a finger to his lips and helps me up onto the porch. He motions to the cabin door. It's heavy, solid wood, and opens with a groan. Sunlight streams into the open room through a small window, illuminating dust particles as they dance in the air. Once we're both inside, he shuts the door behind us and wedges a board across it. I don't really want to think about who—or what—he's trying to keep out.

"That 'thing' is a Conductor."

Conductor.

I shiver. Duke used that word earlier when I teased him about driving a car. He hadn't spoken of them with fear or reverence, the way Oliver does. Maybe Duke had been too young to know better. My heart squeezes when I think of Duke, but I push it aside. I can't take any more pain. "We're not allowed to talk about them?"

"Take a load off." Oliver nods at a rocking chair in the corner. The chair looks old, like it's seen hundreds of better days, happier days. Knitting in the firelight, rocking babies while whispering bedtime stories. I hate to break its streak, but I'm still thankful to settle into the seat and close my eyes.

Beneath the only window sits a table with a white ceramic pitcher and a cluster of dishes resting just out of the sunlight. He pours water into a cloudy glass and holds it out to me. "Here, you must be thirsty." As I take the glass from him, our fingers brush. A tingle of electricity flows between us and travels straight up my arm.

Oliver doesn't move his hand as he studies my face, his lips parted. I almost let the glass fall to the wood floor.

I blush and pull away. "Thanks."

"Back to The Conductors—" He finds a place to sit on the floor, stretching his legs in front of him. "It's not that we can't talk about them, I just wanted to be careful. You nearly got transported there."

"Yeah, about that . . ."

He pauses, staring up at the vaulted peak of the ceiling. "When they take you, that's it. You're not coming back." Oliver's gaze meets mine. "I couldn't let that happen."

The intensity of his eyes is too much and I break the connection. Silence falls around us as I consider all the things I learned today, each bit of knowledge more disturbing than the last. As much as I complained about not knowing Mitte's crazy rules, knowing the truth is worse.

"We're dead." My voice is cool, disconnected from the panic inside. But being dead makes more sense than the alternative.

"No. I'm dead." Oliver pokes his thumb at his chest. "You're . . . I haven't worked out what you are yet, to be honest."

I'm not dead. I should be comforted by this, but I'm not. "Is this Heaven? Because if this is Heaven, I want a refund."

His laugh is bittersweet. "I wish it were."

"Okay, so this is Hell?" Hell feels more like it, the image of The Conductor burned in my brain.

"Not exactly."

"Not Heaven or Hell, and I'm not dead." I bite my lip as I add this up in my mind. When I come up blank, I blurt out, "Are you a zombie?"

It's Oliver's turn to look confused. "A what?"

"A zombie. You know, the living dead." Seriously, who doesn't know what a zombie is? It must be a short list, but Oliver's on it. I sigh. "Oh, never mind. But I gotta ask—do you think brains are a tasty treat?"

He scrunches up his face. "What? Why on earth would you think that?" He shudders. "That's disturbing. You're pretty weird, you know that, Lucy?"

"That's not the first time someone's called me weird." I smile, slowly rocking back and forth in my chair and enjoying its creaky melody. "But you make it sound like a bad thing."

The corners of his mouth twitch upward and the faint light filtering through the window sparkles in his eyes. My stomach flip-flops.

Waitwaitwait! This can't be happening. Oliver just told me he's living-challenged, expired, kaput. News like that should make me shriek and faint, not turn me on. Then again, the last guy to pay any attention to me turned out to be worse than dead. But, Oliver? Dead Oliver?

"You'll stay here tonight."

I shift to the edge of the rocking chair in alarm. "But I . . ."

"Relax. It's only until I talk to the others and make sure you'll be safe again at Miss Perdita's." Rosy patches on his cheeks betray his businesslike tone.

"Oh. Oh yeah, sure."

"You can take the bed, of course." He motions to a crude wooden frame shoved into the back corner of the cabin. "I, uh, don't sleep, so it's all yours."

"You don't sleep? That must suck."

Oliver shakes his head and avoids my eyes. He's still hiding something, I'm sure, but I'm too tired for any more of his revelations. Pointing toward the bed, I ask, "Do you mind?"

He blinks a few times and swallows hard before he speaks. "Not at all," he finally manages, his cheeks flushing again.

I grin as I push myself out of the chair. There's something comforting in the fact that even supernatural Oliver finds this awkward.

Even with the sun streaming through the window, shadows shroud the back of the cabin. I yawn, stretching myself across the bed, not even bothering to pull back the covers. The quilt beneath me is hand-sewn; I trace the uneven lines of thread beneath my fingers and close my eyes. Someone who loved Oliver pieced this blanket together, stitch by stitch by stitch by stitch by . . .

My breathing slows as The Conductors, The Divide, Oliver the Friendly Ghost, and Duke slip away.

Duke.

"Duke's dead," I murmur. Beneath drooping lids, my eyes focus, barely, on Oliver.

"Don't worry about Duke. He'll be right as rain next time you see him." He flashes a tender smile, one I can't help but return.

"Anyone ever tell you that you have a smile that could light up a room?" Oliver says as my eyelids slip shut. "You should smile all the time."

Chapter 13

A low groan wakes me up who-knows-how-many hours later. The night hangs like a heavy curtain, hiding all details of the room around me. My heart thuds toward my throat as I fight to remember where I am. Who I am. What I'm doing here.

There's the sound again. It's coming from outside, this time long and drawn out like a dying breath. Even though I'm freaking out inside, I manage to roll my eyes at how fast I jump to conclusions anymore. Just because Oliver's a— well, just because Oliver's Oliver, and Mitte's Mitte doesn't mean anything. That groan could be anything—the wind howling through a crevice in the crumbling wall. Or maybe a woodland creature that lost a fight with a larger woodland creature.

As I race through the possibilities, I listen for any movement in the darkness. Maybe Oliver isn't so perfect after all and has the world's most disturbing snoring problem. It doesn't have to always be about ghosts and goblins, right?

I mentally reach out for Oliver. There's no way I would really reach for him in a room this dark. Monsters wait for people to stick their arms and legs into the abyss—that's when they gobble them up. I know it's a silly fear left over from ghost stories told at slumber parties and my few excruciating hours at summer camp. Silly or not, after my encounter with The Conductors I'm not taking any chances.

I pull down the quilt, exposing my chin to whatever evil might be lurking in the shadows. "Hey." My words echo too loudly and I wish I could snatch them back up.

No one—or thing—answers.

I suck in a deep breath and try again. "You here?" It's wishful thinking, I know.

Somewhere beyond these walls, a cry rings out—this one shrill and piercing like the grind of metal on metal. My heart dislodges from my throat and sinks towards my toes as another strangled groan rises from the forest beyond these walls.

I don't know how I know it, but I know it as sure as I know anything else—it's Oliver, and he's in trouble.

How many times have I been warned about going outside at night? More than I can count. But I can't just leave him out there by himself, not when I can hear him suffering.

I bite my lip. Stay safe inside, serenaded by Oliver's screams, or wander outside to most likely be captured by The Conductors? *Decisions, decisions.*

For Oliver, this wouldn't be a difficult decision. He'd count it a privilege to jump into the middle of a battle for me. Guys are weird and awesome like that. But what if Oliver can't save himself?

When my bare feet hit the floor and aren't immediately severed from my body, I let out the breath I'd been holding. Inch by inch, I shuffle along the boards, cursing out loud when I bang into the rocking chair with my knee, and again when I get a splinter in the ball of my right foot. I'll have to ask Oliver about the rules on swearing in the Afterworld or whatever Mitte is. My knowledge of the Ten Commandments is pretty rusty beyond "Thou Shalt Not Steal," but I'm not even sure it matters anymore. I'm not dead, or so Oliver says, but it kind of feels like I'm damned anyway.

The cabin door's unlocked. I try not to be offended, but *way to keep me safe, there, buddy.*

I ease the door inward and peek around the edge. The forest lies still as a tomb. No creatures scurry in the shadows or hum in the void. If it wasn't for the whole Demon Task Force, I could almost enjoy camping in a creepy-crawly-free zone.

Oh, yeah. The Conductors. I need to get my head back in the game.

The cover of trees blocks most of the moonlight, making it difficult to see anything more than dark shapes and even darker shapes. Dudes made mostly of flames will be easy to spot in the dark, so at least I have that going for me. Turning a full circle, I find no spawn of Satan. *Good.* To be sure, I tilt my head upward and sniff the gentle breeze. No toxic-sludge fumes assault my nostrils, only the perfume of dew on the leaves. Relieved but still cautious, I creep down the steps. I want to wait and see if Oliver shows up on his own, but standing in the open very long sounds like one of my worst ideas—and, for me, that's saying a lot. Historically, I've made some doozies.

A pained cry shatters the peace of the night. This time I make out a word—*Jasper*—wrung out from the blood-soaked lips of a broken man. I want to crumple into a heap on the ground, remembering the last time I heard anyone speak that way. The last time I heard someone die. But I can't let my own demons win when Oliver might need me.

Instead, I read the forest floor like a passage of Braille, carefully sliding each foot forward before shifting my weight. Foot-slide by painfully-slow foot-slide, I test the dirt in front of me. In another time or place, I could have pretended I was a ninja, relying on my stealth and the gloom of night to keep me safe. I catch my toes on a root snaking its way along my path and launch myself head-first into a bush, dashing my ninja dreams.

"What are you doing?" a voice hisses from the other side of the bush.

I clap my hand over my mouth to keep myself from screaming.

"Get inside," he commands. Even with his volume practically on mute, Oliver's over-protectiveness is unmistakable. It would be irritating, too, if I wasn't so happy to hear him—alive.

"Chill out," I say as I remove myself from the Bush of Broken Ninja Dreams. "I heard you screaming."

"Oh." He pauses. "Sorry. But I'm okay, promise."

He sure hadn't sounded okay, but now that I'm not in a headlock with a shrub I can just barely make out Oliver and Jasper's outlines. Neither one of them seems to need my help.

Confused, we make our way back to the front porch, with Jasper trudging a few steps behind. "I wasn't trying to be sneaky or anything, I swear. I thought something bad had happened to you."

He doesn't answer for a moment. When he finally speaks, his voice is gentle. "Now that you know I'm fine, will you be okay? Till morning, I mean?"

"What time is it?" I ask. The fractured bits of sky visible through the cover of trees remain black as ink, with no hint of the graying before dawn.

"I don't keep track of time. None of us do. To watch the clock in a place like this would drive you insane." His words turn thin and brittle, and I regret asking. "Listen, you really need to get indoors. You're still in danger."

"Okay," I say. "Are you coming with me? I'm not sure I can go back to sleep now."

His sigh fills the space between us. "I can't."

"What do you mean, you can't?"

"Nighttime isn't the same for me, Lucy." His voice trembles like he either wants to snap at me or burst into tears. "I don't get to rest like you do—it's part of the curse of this place."

"So, you can't sleep or whatever . . . Come with me anyway. We can hang out or something." Glancing over my shoulder at his dark form, I rest my hand on the wooden door and nudge it inward with my palm. The hinges squeal in protest and I wince, immediately pulling away.

"Even if I could go with you, I wouldn't."

"Why not?"

"I—I sure would feel better if you'd just get inside and shut the door."

"Not without you. I'm kind of freaked out, especially since it's so dark."

"All the more reason for me to stay away."

He's so ridiculously frustrating with all this secrecy. If I thought it would make me feel better, I'd wring his neck for all the games he plays. "Please, don't leave me alone here. I never thought I'd hear myself say this to you, of all people, but I'm begging you to stay with me."

"Lucy, if it were up to me, I'd stay with you every second of every day."

My heart thuds again in my throat at his words, and I swallow hard to send it back to its rightful place in my chest. "If it's not up to you, then who is it up to?"

I don't need him to answer my question and he doesn't try. Whoever's in charge here has already left their mark on me, a handprint seared into my arm and a blistering line running down toward my neck. If The Conductors don't make the rules, they at least enforce them. That gives them as much authority as anybody around here, I guess.

Oliver has done so much to keep me safe so far. The last thing I want is to lure The Conductors here to his front porch. Not when a few steps will put an inch of wood between me and evil.

"Well, see you when I see you, then," I say as I slip into the cabin.

Oliver's reply is the fade of hoofbeats into the brush. I immediately miss him, which makes no sense to me. Maybe I miss him because the darkness of Mitte holds such terror, and I want him to be around to save me from it. Or maybe the unthinkable has happened and I actually care for him in some way. Whatever the reason, my body feels heavier with him gone. Without Oliver, all of this feels hopeless.

Shutting the door behind me with a clunk, I lean against the gnarled wood and rest my palm on my forehead. Too many thoughts swirl in my brain, and I shake my head to break them apart. If only it was that easy.

Smoke curls around me, and I bolt upright in bed. Fear bursts within my chest, my eyes wide and desperate. I don't know how long I slept, but judging by the sunbeams filtering through the window, it was too long. The Conductors are probably waiting outside, ready to transfer me or whatever, and I've almost missed it. Yeah, I'm so tricky I've overslept for my own execution. Just my luck.

I peek out the window, but the angle's all wrong for spotting anyone out front. Acid rises in my throat as I consider my options: hide out forever in the cabin, or square my jaw like a brave little soldier and surrender.

This one time, Tanya made me watch a movie where the evil spirits couldn't cross over a line of salt—or maybe sugar—on the floor. Maybe these flimsy walls are enough to hold off Satan's sidekicks, but I'm not feeling too confident about the cabin's chances against beings made entirely out of fire. Holing myself up here will only buy me time until the inevitable.

Shoot. Brave little soldier it is.

If The Conductors are going to try to lay their hands on me, I'll need something to protect me from their burning touch. My gaze darts around the small room, searching for something to cover my skin, but there's not much here. Not even a stitch of clothing hangs in the open closet. Ghosts apparently don't have a problem with wearing the same old thing day after day. It cuts down on laundry, which is definitely a bonus, but seems pretty boring. And, currently, it's pretty inconvenient for me. With a sigh, I slide the delicate quilt from Oliver's bed and wrap it around my body. The yellowed fabric is like a familiar touch against my skin. Oliver's mother or grandmother probably spent a great deal of time stitching the pieces together by hand, perhaps even as they rocked in the very chair in the center of his cabin. If I turn his family heirloom into a pile of ashes, I hope he can find it in his heart to forgive me. I just can't let those . . . *things* . . . brand me again.

I hesitate at the door. If I catch The Conductors off guard, I can still try to outrun them. Not that long ago, I could shoot out of the blocks like a rocket. My ankle aches and my hip will never be the same after the surgeons welded me back together, but if I need to run to escape danger maybe I can force all the parts to work together. Besides, how fast can a bunch of dudes on fire really be?

Okay, dumb question. Forget I asked.

Wrapped in the comforter like a caterpillar burrowed in its cocoon, I take a deep breath to quell my nausea and shuffle to the door. By facing my fear, even the fear of certain death, I am evolving into something stronger than I was hours, even minutes, before. First, though, I curse Oliver for not installing a peephole for his stupid, creaky door. With one last gulp of air, I throw it open. What happens next needs to happen fast— no reason to drag it out.

"Good morning, sunshine," Oliver says, stabbing at a crackling fire with a long iron poker.

I furrow my eyebrows. "The . . ." Can I speak their name out loud or not? "You know, those things that nearly killed me yesterday. They're not here?"

"No, they aren't. Why would you think that?" It's his turn to look confused.

Relief washes over me, and I let the quilt fall loose around my shoulders. "The smoke woke me up."

"Sorry about that. I reckon you must be hungry."

A row of hot dogs sizzles and pops on a rack above the fire and my mouth waters. Yesterday I'd been planning on eating ice cream—chocolate chip!—with the kids, but obviously that hadn't worked out. I'm hungry, which is the only thing I'm sure about anymore.

The morning air is growing thick and damp already, so I toss the quilt inside the cabin door before joining him.

Using a long fork, Oliver rolls the hot dogs over to make sure they cook evenly. Hot dogs seem like a pretty modern food choice for an old soul, but nothing about him can possibly surprise me more than finding out who he really is. What he really is.

I watch him work in silence, admiring the flash of flames in the liquid of his eyes. "Do you eat?" I ask, finally.

"Sure. But I don't need to."

My stomach growls. "Must be nice to be able to choose."

He arranges four hot dog buns on the wire rack above the fire, seeming to arrange his thoughts as he does. "People get stuck doing the same ol' thing day after day—eating, working, loving, losing. When we die, a lot of things die with us. But those of us who are stuck don't have a whole lot to be happy for, so we try to remember what made us happy before. Most of us love a good meal."

"When you say 'good meal,' does that *really* include hot dogs?" I joke.

"What's wrong with hot dogs? Everyone loves hot dogs!"

"My mom wouldn't let me ea—" I stop myself short at the thought of my mother. I miss her, even her crazy obsession with ridding the house of processed food.

We sit in silence for a few minutes until Oliver swipes a toasted bun from the rack and fills it with a plump hot dog. With a wink, he hands it off to me. "What your mama don't know won't hurt her. Dig in."

A bag near Oliver's feet holds little packets of ketchup, mustard, and relish (ick!). I grab a handful of ketchup packets and sink to the ground several feet back from the fire. Using my teeth, I tear into one of the packets and squirt a zigzag of red onto my dog. The routine of prepping my meal is so boring, so normal, in a place where nothing is normal. It's comforting.

I chew and swallow a bite before I gather enough courage for my next question. "Everyone here is dead?"

When I look to him, his gaze is lost deep within the dance of the flames, his mouth pulled in a thin line. My answer—to that question, at least. I have loads more.

"My family isn't—wasn't—real religious." I hesitate. "But I've always been taught that when you, uh, *die,* you either go up or you go down."

I haven't even reached the question and tension already hums from Oliver's body. *Do I really want to know?*

He clenches his jaw, waiting for me to continue.

Yes, I do want to know, especially if it means I'll understand. "If all of that's true, then why did you end up here?"

He turns his sad eyes to mine.

Chapter 14

Regret.

Something holds each person in Mitte captive like chains around their ankles. Something they wished they'd been able to do in life, something they wished to change. The more I think about it, the more the pieces fall into place. Miss Millie hadn't been able to feed the family she worked for, so she watched them wither away before her eyes. Vera, the waitress at Sal's Diner, stole from her friend but hadn't been able to make it right while her heart still beat in her chest. These people carried such guilt and pain with them to the grave—and now, beyond.

My life overflows with things I wish I could have done differently, so it makes a lot of sense for me to be stuck in this kind of purgatory. Except

Oliver's sure I'm not dead. Maybe death had messed with his mind and he's confused. Death, I get. Still being alive and losing everything—that doesn't make one ounce of sense.

When I ask Oliver why he's stuck in Mitte, he stops talking. I've pushed him too far, and I know it. After we finish our meal, I wander away to give him a little space.

I don't really want to know all their stories, I decide as I amble through the forest. I can't even handle my own crap. Taking on more than that will crush me.

But, then, why am I here?

When I get back to the cabin, Oliver's put out the fire with a bucket of water. My skin crawls at the sizzle of the protesting embers and the cloud of smoke, reminders of The Conductors. I shudder and wrap my arms around myself as I lower to the edge of the porch.

Oliver must have noticed my shiver, because he sits down beside me and hands me a coffee mug.

"Careful," he warns. "It's hot."

I dare to take the tiniest of sips, my taste buds jerking in shock at the heat. Hot chocolate.

Even in the shade of the pines, the temperature soars and the thickness of the air plasters my clothes to my body. A warm drink is an odd choice. But, hey, it's Oliver. *Odd* barely scratches the surface.

"Hot cocoa makes everyone feel better. It's like home in a cup," he says.

I'd never really thought about it before, but he's right. With each cautious sip, the memories flood back.

Christmas Eve, nestled on the couch with my parents, a fire crackling in the fireplace. Some years, the weather would cooperate, sending snow to the ground like countless feathers outside the picture window. Other years, we sat on the couch, hopeful for a change in luck. Dad always insisted Mom and I unwrap a small gift while we cuddled there; he loved to give his girls gifts so much that his impatience won out one year. The tradition stuck; same with Mom's roses.

All of that from a cup of cocoa. I blink down at the murky liquid, and then to Oliver. His thoughts seem a million miles away, even though he's staring at the patch sewn to the knee of his pants.

I fiddle with the tail of my scarf. "What was your home like?"

Snapped back into the present, he nods toward the cabin. "You're looking at it."

My mouth twitches. By *home*, I hadn't meant the actual building, but I guess I need to be more specific. "Cool, but what about your family?"

"I had an older brother, Martin; and a little sister, Agatha. And, of course, my Ma and Pop."

"All of you fit in that tiny space?"

"There used to be a loft; that's where us children slept. My parents used the bed where you spent last night," he said.

"There used to be a loft? What happened to it?"

Oliver returns to staring at his knee. He picks at an errant stitch on the corner of the patch. "I took it down. I couldn't bear to look at it anymore after . . ." His mouth clamps shut. I don't need to ask if something awful had taken place here. The answer reflects in the slope of his shoulders and the droop of his expression. His response is familiar, down to him clearing his throat and brushing away a tear before anyone else gets a good look. We're more alike than I first thought.

He rubs his face with his callused hands and exhales. "I haven't thought about any of that in a real long time. No offense, but I'm not about to start now."

I blink in surprise. "Uh, okay. Forget I asked."

With a nod, he accepts this and moves on. His eyes, normally sparkling and mischievous, are hollow and haunted. Doc Blevins said that Oliver still has hope, which I didn't really understand at the time. I'm not sure I really get it now, honestly. But now that his smile's gone, I miss it. His warmth really is the most hopeful thing in this place. Without it, my heart aches with enough force to almost wring itself in two.

I like him. I really, really like him.

No, I don't. Guys are evil.

Then why is Oliver getting to me so bad? My palms are sweating and everything.

Hello! It's like a billion degrees out and I'm drinking hot chocolate. My whole body is drenched. If I like him, it's by default. He's the only guy my age here.

But I don't like him—and I won't—because I won't let another guy get close. Not after stupid Derek. I wasn't even trying to be with that colossal jerk and he still ruined my life. Right now Oliver's nothing like Derek, true; but give him time.

Do I really believe that?

Almost as if he's listening in on my crazy inner debate, Oliver looks up from his mug. His inky hair falls over one eye, and my fingers long to reach out and brush it to the side so both of his eyes can focus their intensity on mine. I imagine the feel of his skin beneath my touch, running from his temple to his jaw, where he . . .

I jump to my feet, ignoring the stab of pain that shoots down my spine. "Let's go somewhere," I say. We can't sit still anymore, not if I expect to keep myself from Oliver.

The tension holding us together in the moment snaps like a rubber band stretched beyond its limits. Frowning, he leans away. *He felt the connection, too. I'm sure of it.*

"Okay." He reaches toward me and my gaze drops to his outstretched hand. After a frozen moment, he stands and closes the distance between us.

My mouth dries up and I struggle to swallow. Our eyes connect, and I can't breathe.

This is it. I don't know what it is, but this is it.

Oliver grabs the mug from me, his fingers whispering against mine, then dumps the last little bit of hot chocolate onto the ground. "Where do you want to go?"

I shrug, trying to push against the magnetic pull between us. Beneath my skin, my pulse thunders out of control like a herd of mustangs.

What's happening to me?

I force a smile for Oliver. "I dunno. What do you usually do during the day—I mean, when you're not rescuing me and stuff?"

"I take care of the roses, but you're probably not interested in helping with that in this heat."

Even standing still, the sweat beads on my forehead and right above my upper lip. What I really want is a tall glass of lemonade and a hammock in the shade, or, even better, air conditioning and a cool shower. Since that's out of the question until Oliver takes me back to Aunt Perdita's, there aren't a whole lot of other options.

One thing I know for sure—I can't stay at the cabin with him any longer with nothing to distract me from, well, *him.*

"Roses!" I blurt, interrupting the path my thoughts were following. My face heats up and I try again. "What I *meant* was that I'd be happy to help you with the roses. Fair warning, though—I have a black thumb. I kill everything I touch." My heavy words fall to the ground. Of course I hadn't meant it like that, but I can't argue with their truth.

Oliver offers the faintest trace of a smile at my slip. "I'm not worried, Luce."

I'm not sure if he's referring to the roses or something else, but he's gone back to being cryptic. Cryptic is normal and way less romantic. Yes, cryptic will work. I nod my approval to myself, and Oliver raises an eyebrow at me.

Heat rises to my cheeks. "Never mind," I mumble. His smile deepens, and I look away before my heart accelerates any more.

"Let me get Jasper, then." He sets off toward his horse.

Jasper. My heart beats faster, and this time it has nothing to do with my tall, dark, and handsome friend. Acid rolls in the pit of my stomach as I watch the big spotted horse search the forest floor for grass. He lifts his long neck and stares at me as he chews, his round jaw flexing.

"Really, Oliver. It's okay. My ankle's feeling a lot better, see? I can walk." I take a few steps forward, showing off how awesome and normal my ankle is. I nearly bite the tip of my tongue off from the pain, but I'd rather drag myself across the forest using only my hands than willingly climb back on that demon-possessed horse again. As if on cue, my ankle rolls, and I stumble to the side. I catch myself and take another step sideways to make it look like I meant to do that, but Oliver isn't buying it. Once Jasper is saddled, Oliver walks him straight up to me and holds out the reins.

My mouth drops open. "Whatever you're thinking, *no*." To me, Jasper holds an unknown capacity for deadly scenarios—though it seems his specialty is smooshing his passengers. I'm sure a plethora of other dangers lurks unseen beneath his adorable, horsey exterior. He doesn't fool me for a second.

"Now, hear me out," Oliver says. "Jasper's a good horse, but he's scared of The Conductors, just like any sensible creature should be. He didn't mean to throw you those times, and he'd like to make it up to you."

"No." I cross my arms. Not only am I not interested in the horse, but I'm kind of questioning his delusional owner, too.

Oliver ignores me. "I got to thinkin', because you're a strong girl—excuse me, strong *lady*—that maybe you're scared because you can't control Jasper. Today we change that."

I continue staring him down.

"If you try it and you hate it, I won't ask again. Swear."

Sometime during his last sentence or two, I lost track of the conversation. I hadn't lost track of the movement of his mouth, though.

"Deal?"

"Sure," I breathe. I'm not entirely sure what I've agreed to; all I can think of is his lips, my lips, our lips together. *Lips, lips, lips. What's wrong with me all of a sudden? Did he slip some kind of voodoo love potion into that hot chocolate?*

Before I can change my mind, Oliver hoists me into the saddle and adjusts the stirrups so I'll feel more secure on the big gelding's back. Patiently, he places his callused hand on mine to show me how moving the reins against Jasper's neck asks him to turn in a certain direction. My skin tingles under his touch, like there's an electric current running between us. It takes me longer to learn than it should because I make him repeat everything two or three times. He doesn't seem to mind one bit; even when I've obviously done something well, he repeats the instruction again. It's like he wants an excuse to touch me. Don't get me wrong, I'm not complaining.

Then his fingers run along my calf as he discusses how to ask Jasper to walk, and I about leap off the horse and into his arms. That's saying a lot about my pull to Oliver, since flying off a horse again isn't high on my list of favorite activities. I don't understand what's going on with my own body and why I'm responding to handsome but infuriating Oliver this way.

"We'll take it slow, for now," he says as our eyes meet. "Only walking."

A knot forms in the pit of my stomach when I realize he's only talking about horses. I swallow, trying to force down the lump in my throat, and smile back at him. "Slow's good."

"Slow it is," he replies. His grin slips behind an expression I can't place, and his hand lingers on the outside of my knee longer than necessary. I suck in a sharp breath when his thumb feathers across my bare skin.

We're still talking about horses, right?

Without a word, Oliver swings onto Jasper's back and shimmies into place behind the saddle. We're not as close as when we rode Jasper bareback, but, still, the heat of Oliver's body prickles along my back. And when he brushes the top of my knee with his fingertips, prompting me to nudge the horse into movement, I can almost feel his amusement. The boy knows just what he's doing to me.

Once I get the hang of steering Jasper and learn how to steady him down steeper inclines, I find that I'm no longer as scared to ride. Oliver had been right about that—I just needed more control. Jasper still has a mind of his own, but he obeys me when I ask for something, which I respect. He doesn't listen to me because I possess some kind of natural talent, but because he has a gentle spirit. A gentle spirit that likes to dump me in the dirt every once in a while, but whatever.

Not only do I feel more control when Oliver hands the reins over to me, but I notice something else, too. Sitting tall in Jasper's saddle as we walk along mimics the sensation of walking, something I haven't been able to do without a limp in months. On Jasper's back, my hips rock back and forth, side to side. It's so strange and so familiar, all at the same time. Best of all, there's no pain, which is something I haven't been able to say in forever. I can't help the tears that well up in the corner of my eyes.

"Is everything okay?" Oliver asks.

"This is amazing. Thank you for not listening to me."

He laughs softly. "You're welcome, I think."

"Riding Jasper reminds me of running," I explain. "Running was the one thing I was really good at before the accident, but now it's gone."

"I'm sorry."

"Me too," I say. "But it's nice to remember how I felt before, so, that's . . . good."

We ride quietly for a while before he feels the need to speak again. "Can I ask you something?" He fumbles his words, like he's wrestling with the courage to speak them.

Even though I'm pretty sure I don't want to answer him, I shrug. "All right."

"Well, I've been trying to figure out why you're here. What happened to you, Lucy?"

I take a deep breath to steady myself. No one has ever asked me what happened. Sure, they asked about the accident—I figured to file police reports and insurance claims and otherwise place the blame firmly on my shoulders without saying those exact words. No one had ever asked about *me*.

"It's a really long story. You sure?"

Oliver squeezes my hip in response. And, one by one, the ghosts appear.

Chapter 15

"You're not like the others." He grins, zeroing in on me with his intense emerald eyes.

Those are totally contacts. Between that and his gigantic dimples, I don't trust his eyes to be that bright. Let's face it—nobody's genetics are that generous.

"Excuse me?" I look over my shoulder, still not sure he's actually talking to me.

Derek Carver slides across the couch until he's so close the fabric of his designer jeans rubs against my bare thigh. I shrink away from the sensation, a little bit skeeved out by his hovering. What on earth does Tanya see in him, anyway? Besides the fact that he's ridiculously good-looking and captain of the football team, I mean. For someone who's supposed to be dating my best friend, Derek sure seems to be getting pretty friendly with me. Call me old-fashioned or whatever, but cheating is kind of a turn-off.

He delivers his line again. "I said that you're not like the other girls, Lisa."

"It's Lucy," I say. "And am I really that different? I hadn't noticed."

"Lucy! That's right," he booms, as if I'm rating how sorry he is based on volume alone. "Forgive me for being such a jerk?"

I shrug, leaning away from him to give myself the tiniest bit of personal space.

His meaty paw is on my knee before I can react. "You're sexy, you know that?"

I squeak out a laugh, scanning the room from one wall to the other. Where's the hidden camera? No way is this happening for real. Guys like Derek don't go for girls like me, number one. Number two, even if I wanted his attention, he's completely off-limits. Tanya wouldn't hesitate to rip out the hair of any girl stupid enough to exchange words with one of her boyfriends; and, honestly, I love my hair too much to risk it.

But here I sit, smack dab in the middle of what's sure to be a fight with my best friend tomorrow. No one will bother to tell her I'd been pinned against the corner of the couch like a scared animal—that's not how rumors spread. By tomorrow night the story would morph into us ripping each other's clothes off in the middle of Manny's party.

I roll my eyes as Derek's hand slides upward, trying to keep my cool but freaking out inside. Dad had taken one look at me and told me to change when I started toward the door in my pale-yellow sundress, but I had dismissed him with a sweet smile and a peck on the cheek. Now I wish I'd listened.

I push away Derek's searching hand with as much force as I can. He whimpers in protest, his sloppy mouth breathing heavily in my ear. It smells like a bottle of vodka up and died inside of him. Derek Carver is 110% wasted.

People watch us from all around the room, and I try to connect with any of them for a little help, por favor! But as my pleading eyes meet theirs, they turn away. Suddenly that conversation with their buddy is a lot more interesting. None of Derek's lackeys want to turn on him—they've got their social standing to think about. Thanks, guys. I'm totally fine here under 175 pounds of misguided hormones.

If only Tanya had given in when I'd begged her to come with me to the afterparty, then Derek would be all up in her business instead of manhandling me. None of the rumors at school on Monday morning would be about me, at least. But, nooo . . . She had to go and catch the flu and leave me here with Mr. Grabbyhands. I'm calling *her first thing in the morning to tell her to dump this loser—that is, if he doesn't suffocate me first.*

"Lulu," Derek slurs.

"Lucy."

"That's what I said," he insists, showing every single one of his pearly whites. "Liesl."

"Now you're just making it up."

"You know who you are and you know you want to take this party somewhere more . . . pirate," he says. His hooded eyes swim way too close to mine. In case I haven't caught his meaning, he brings his foul mouth back to my ear and proceeds to stick his nasty tongue in there. Ewww. Who does that?

As enticing as his slobber is in my ear-hole, I've had enough. "It's 'private,' you moron. And you seriously need to get off of me right now."

Derek's onslaught to my ear moves down the side of my neck. Reflexes kick in and I pinch his face between my shoulder and head. Apparently that move activates his aggression button, and he drives my upper body against the arm of the couch with his entire bodyweight.

"Stop fighting it, babe," he says through gritted teeth. "You know you want to."

So cliché. So absolutely terrifying.

It's my turn to get right in his ear. "If you don't get away from me right now I will personally make sure you never have children."

He pulls away, only far enough to look me in the eyes to judge my sincerity. Inside, I'm trembling like a frightened child, but my outsides fix him with an icy glare. I cannot afford to be a weak girl right now. Not if I want to escape Derek Carver with my dignity intact.

"Try me. See if I'm kidding." My tone is full of acid, dead serious. Derek studies me for what feels like an hour before he releases me.

He sneers. "Your loss." Like that'll convince me to change my mind. Nonchalantly, he moves one of his giant hands forward to protect his crotch. He took me seriously. Good.

A guy near the kitchen doorway calls for Derek. He says his name twice before Derek turns his attention away from me. "Busy, bro," he says, pointing to me.

"Doesn't look like she's that into you," the other guy answers. I can't see him, but whoever it is deserves a pat on the back for being the only chivalrous one in the room.

"Bro. You really need to go do something else," Derek says. "Or someone else."

"You too," mystery guy fires back. "Leave her alone."

Derek snorts. "Whatever, dude. She's so not worth it." To stick it to me one last time, he snakes around and raises his voice. "You hear me? You're. Not. Worth. It." With that, he shrinks away from me like a wounded animal going off to lick its oozing injuries. It's probably the first time he's ever been rejected, even with his less-than-smooth courting techniques. I wish that made me feel even a little better about what had just happened and what could have happened if the guy from the other side of the room hadn't stood up to the god of our high school.

Even though I don't recognize the guy who saved me from Derek, there's something so familiar about him. His dark hair, eyes the color of the earth. It triggers a memory—déjà vu, maybe—but I push it away. I've never met him before.

When I brush past him on my way toward the door, he doesn't say anything. Our eyes meet, the only thing I can manage in way of a thank-you. I hope he knows I'm grateful. He blinks back, then bows his head to take a sip from a bottle of water.

After searching the entire house, I find my friend Lisette snoring near a puddle of vomit in Manny's bathroom. Correct me if I'm wrong, but it's probably a party foul to pass out in a bathtub when you're someone else's ride. Even though I'm not drinking, unlike most everyone else at Manny's, I don't have a car or a license. I'm stranded, unless I want to call my parents for a ride, and I don't.

Mystery Man In the Living Room was drinking water. That water bottle, not a red plastic cup, pegged him as a designated driver, the one who drew the short straw for the evening's festivities. With a sigh, I drag myself back into the living room to beg my nameless hero another favor—my safe delivery home.

The next morning my phone buzzes into life hours before I plan on waking up. It's Tanya. She must have heard about Derek's bad behavior and wants to let me know she's finally dropped him. I'm not ready for what's sure to be a conversation full of waterworks, so I turn my phone off and go back to sleep. Tanya, on the other hand, feels it's so important we talk that she comes over to do it in person.

She looks like crap, I notice as I peek at her through the peephole. Worse than that—more like crap that's been run over a few times. Her short, dark braids stand up all over her head like she'd tossed and turned all night, and her face backs that up. Shadows outline her usually bright hazel eyes, which are bloodshot. That flu must be pretty awful, because she's definitely had better days. Why in the world would she come around here if she felt half as bad as she looks? I, for sure, don't want it. There's literally nothing worse than yakking.

Sucking in a breath so I can avoid her cloud of germs, I unlock the door. "Hey, what's up?"

Tanya answers me with a slap across the face.

"Wh-what was that for?" I cry, my hand flying to my cheek. It stings like fire where she made contact, and I'm pretty sure there will be a hand-shaped welt there later. Tears spring to my eyes, and I blink to clear them just in case I have to dodge another blow. Her assault on me is delayed by her sudden need to throw up all over Mom's azalea bush.

"How could you?" she asks, wiping her mouth with the back of her sleeve, which is totally gross. Her shoulders hunch and she looks wild.

My mouth hangs open, not sure what she's accusing me of.

"You slept with him!" She doesn't wait for me to confirm or deny anything. "I was sick as a dog and you saw that as your big chance to steal my boyfriend."

This is about loser-head? I want to leave Tanya seething on my stoop, drive over to Derek's mansion, and make good on last night's threat to neuter him unless he clears this up. Excessive, maybe, but Tanya is surprisingly strong for a girl who probably weighs a hundred pounds soaking wet. Had Coach been training her for shot put or something when I wasn't watching?

Tanya takes my silence as admission and lurches toward me, almost connecting to my jaw with one of her flailing fists. Tears stream down her cheeks, and I know she's hurting. Not slap-to-the-face hurting, but hurting all the same.

"Wait," I cry, throwing my hands up to protect my face from her blind attack. "Tanya, quit!"

She doesn't listen, advancing on me until my back presses against the door. "You knew I really liked him, and that we were going to get married and—"

I laugh. Like, literally, out loud. None of this is funny, but I can't help it. Derek seemed very concerned with his white-picket-fence dream last night while feeling me up in the middle of Manny's party.

"—have kids! But that didn't stop you from spreading your legs, you bi—"

Before she can finish telling me exactly what she thinks of me and where she believes I should go, the door flies inward and I fall on my butt on the rug just inside the door. My mom stares down at me with her forehead furrowed in concern. She glances over at Tanya, who's ready to self-combust in her state of rage, and then back to me as I scramble to my feet.

"Is there a problem, girls?" Mom asks warily. "I heard a lot of racket and—"

"No," I snap, dusting off my backside.

Tanya smiles at my mom, but her lower lip quivers. "No problem, other than your precious daughter having sex with my future husband."

"What?" Mom says, but I ignore her.

"What-EVER, Tanya." I snort. "He is not going to marry you, and, if you want my opinion, that's the best thing to never happen—"

"Yeah, I really don't want your opinion, you homewrecker."

I roll my eyes. Ugh, she's so dramatic. "I didn't sleep with anyone. Your 'boyfriend'—" I use my fingers to make air quotes, "—was blitzed out of his freaking mind."

"That's not what Kelly and Sarah and everyone at the party said. And, believe me, I called, like, everyone." As crazy as she's acting right now, I believe she had called, like, everyone. There's a little part of me that feels satisfaction in knowing all the tools who hadn't bothered to save me from Derek's unwanted attention had been jarred from their hangovers by Tanya's screeching insanity.

Mom, who had been mostly silent up until this point, puts her hand on my shoulder and spins me so we're eye-to-eye. "You're having sex? And drinking?" Her voice spans several octaves in very few words, which means I'm about to be in big trouble.

I practically die right there, on the spot. "What? Mom! No!"

Turning to Tanya, who quickly wipes a smug look off her face, Mom says, "Tanya, dear, I think you'd better go home. Do you need a ride? You don't look like you're feeling well."

Dear? I wince at her words. My own mother has turned against me.

"I'll be just fine, Mrs. Torres, but thank you." As she speaks, Tanya's eyes never leave mine. Something tells me she's gotten the last word in our friendship, but the last laugh will be on her when she finds out Derek's a lying, cheating scumbag. Bonus points if she also later discovers I was completely innocent and it makes her feel like a really horrible person.

"You're sure?" Mom arches an eyebrow as Tanya heaves over top of the bush again. "A glass of water, perhaps?"

"Mom, she said she's fine. She's always right." I meet Tanya's weak glare with my own. I don't even understand what's happening here. Once I bury myself up to my armpits in chocolate chip ice cream and mull it all over, I'm pretty sure I still won't understand.

Mom and I watch in silence as Tanya hurls once more in the gutter next to her car before driving off. My insides feel utterly numb except for the urge to shower Tanya's germs from my body and possibly inhale some disinfectant while I'm at it. I trudge toward my bathroom, still in denial, when Mom clears her throat.

"Not so fast, Lucille."

Lucille. No one, not even my parents, is allowed to call me Lucille. With my back turned, I feel safe letting my eyes roll. If she caught me doing something so disrespectful to her face, it would be the last trip my eyes would take. I sigh and turn to her, crossing my arms and steadying myself for what's coming next: punishment for a crime I didn't commit.

Vivid details refresh in my mind of Derek's clammy hand groping the ticklish skin on my thigh, the way his hot breath on my neck froze the blood in my veins—the feeling of danger. Derek's stinky, slimy tongue in my ear was punishment enough, and would haunt me for eternity—longer than any grounding Mom has in mind, I'm pretty sure.

"I can explain . . ." I start.

Deep lines etch her normally warm face as she points down the hall. "In the living room, young lady."

With a heavy sigh, I drag myself into the living room. Dad has his feet up on the coffee table, engrossed in highlights from the World Cup soccer playoffs. He slides his feet from the table *before Mom can yell at him. Taking a sip of coffee, he tips his head toward the TV. "Morning, girls. Manchester's really whooping on everyone this year." Neither Mom nor I follow soccer, but I give him the tiniest of smiles to show my support for Manchester—whoever or whatever that is.*

Mom sits down next to him on the couch, and I plop on the floor to sit Indian-style. I'm not interested in sitting in one of the wingback armchairs where I'd feel like I was on trial. Like I'd done something wrong. My face scrunches up, irritated by the whole situation. She still hasn't let me say a word. No, Tanya was the only one who'd been allowed to speak.

Mom grabs the remote and mutes the television, now partially hidden by my head. "Well, Tanya just stopped by," she begins. I don't like the tone of her voice at all. It's the one she saves for particularly troublesome gossip. Through the years, Dad has grown numb to the nuances of her voice, and he doesn't seem to take the hint that he should show more concern.

He takes another sip of coffee and reaches across her for the remote so he can unmute the TV. "Mm-hmm."

"John! Would you pay attention to me?"

The shrillness of her voice cuts through his fog, and he blinks twice. It's like Mom pulled him out of stand-by mode or something. "So, what about Tanya?" He nods toward the flat-screen. "If we could wrap this up during the commercial break, that'd be great."

If looks could kill and I had anything to say about it, Mom would be the one on trial, not me. Frowning, Dad puts one palm up in surrender. "Fine. I'll record it or something."

Now, if you were a stranger who just happened to meet my family at this particular moment in time, you'd think we aren't particularly close or that we really don't get along. Maybe you would think my parents are strict and unfair. If you thought any of those things, you'd be dead wrong. We aren't perfect in any way, shape, or form, but we love each other. I've always felt like I could come to my parents with my problems, like getting slapped in the face and cussed out by my seriously misinformed best friend. Still, my parents are only human. And today they're screwing it up. Big-time.

"Lucy, honey, I think it's time your dad and I talked to you about—" She gulps. "—Sex."

I jump to my feet. "You've gotta be kidding me."

Mom's eyes dart toward the door like she's cursing herself for not barricading me in here until she finishes. I'd gone to state finals the last two years as a sprinter, so the odds of her getting there before me are slim. But if I run from them now, I know it's only a matter of time before she *corners me again. I sigh and sink to the floor again.*

For the longest half-hour of my entire life, my mother goes through the birds and the bees talk. She's serious, too. I try to interrupt to remind her that I took Sex Ed. in middle school—she'd signed the permission slip and everything—so I know what parts go where and why. She shushes me then leaves the room, only to return with a banana and a foil packet. Swear to God, I almost make a break for the door again.

She tears away the edge of the wrapper with her teeth and must have picked up on the look of horror on my face. "Luce, hon. I know this is uncomfortable for all of us, but we want to make sure you're being safe." Not Dad. Clearly the look on his face says he wants to be anywhere else but here, never to speak of this day ever again. I would have thought he was sleeping with his eyes open or something if he hadn't kept asking me Derek's name, like he's plotting a rather grisly murder, which is fine by me.

Just kidding.

But, seriously, go ahead, Dad.

Mom, on the other hand, needs to cut it out.

"Oh my gosh, Mom," I groan, burying my face in my hands. "Will you let me talk? This whole—" I gesture toward the piece of fruit in her hand. "—thing is totally unnecessary."

She offers a weak smile, looking relieved. "That's really great, dear. I'm glad you're being safe."

If it's possible for a person to explode out of sheer frustration, well, I'm nearing the danger zone. The blood in my veins bubbles beneath the surface, and tension grows within each of my finely-tuned muscles.

My parents are cool. My parents are cool. My parents are cool. Maybe if I repeat it enough times it will be true again.

I try to erase every awkward sentence—which is most of them—from my memory. When Mom has me practice unrolling the condom onto the banana, I almost hyperventilate. But most of all, I'm angry.

"I keep trying to tell you guys—I didn't sleep with anyone," I force through gritted teeth after throwing the banana across the room, where it lands on my dad's lap. He jumps and blinks rapidly, waking from the coma he'd put himself in during the whole birds and bees bit.

"Tanya's boyfriend, or whatever he is, was all over me at Manny's. There's no way I would have actually slept with him."

"Okay, whatever you say." The words sound sincere enough, but Mom's expression still holds doubt.

I take that as my cue to make myself scarce, to give all of us some space. To find someone who believes I'm pure and innocent. And that is no one.

Seventeen years old and I still haven't taken my driving test at the DMV. I think I'm the only one I know who's still a little—okay, a lot—scared to have that much responsibility. My own two feet are so much more reliable, and I don't have to think twice about pedals or knobs or blinkers if I need to stop or swerve around another runner. Cars crash, and when they do, the injuries are worse than scraped knees and muscle strains. It's some sort of rite of passage I don't quite get—I mean, there's a bus stop every corner or so, it seems. If I can't reach it by bus, I probably don't need to go there anyway. Of course, my parents disagree with that logic. They forced me to agree to take a driving test next week, and because of it, they're insisting I drive everywhere to get in a little more practice.

"Won't it be so nice when you can drive home from your practices and your meets and . . ." Mom's voice drifts off, probably daydreaming of how my license will free up unlimited hours in her week to do whatever it is that Mom likes to do.

I grunt in response.

"You remember how to get to Bellissimo, right?"

Another grunt. We'd eaten our weekly Sunday night dinners as a family at the same restaurant for at least three years. Pretty sure I can figure it out.

"Turn right here. Don't forget about the stop sign," she instructs from the passenger seat. From the corner of my eye, I catch her hand as it clutches the door handle. I can't see it, but I know she's mashing an imaginary brake pedal beneath her sandals when I don't come to a stop as quickly as she would have liked.

"Mom, chill."

After The Most Annoying and Awkward Parental Lecture Ever, I'd spent the afternoon holed up in my room. Luckily my parents had taken the hint and left me alone to read and watch movies, my chosen distraction from the soap opera my life had transformed into overnight. Now that I'm trapped in the car with them, the weight of their accusations presses on me. My muscles ache as I grip the steering wheel, and my jaw throbs from clenching my teeth.

We're on the main road now, only a mile or so from the restaurant. Traffic is unusually heavy, and it takes a lot of my concentration to figure out how fast I can go and how hard I need to push the brake to keep from rear-ending the cars turning ahead.

Out of the blue, Mom announces, "I think we should talk to your doctor about birth control."

My mind goes blank. What?

Ahead lays an intersection, one I only need to proceed straight through. The light's green, which is lucky because I'm burning from the inside out. Bellissimo's so close I can smell roasted garlic drifting in through the air-conditioning vent. If we don't get there soon, where I can free myself from the burden of Mom's disbelief, my head will literally explode. There's only so long a girl can hold off her teenage angst, ya know? Just a little bit further.

"Lucy. LUCY, SLOW DOWN!"

Mom's frantic tone cuts through my thoughts, and, out of the corner of my eye I notice her clawing at her seat with her fingernails. The green light had turned to yellow, with red soon to follow. A wave of panic washes over me, but instead of following her directions, I glare over at her.

"Mom, chill out. I know!" I lash out. "Stop treating me like a child."

She's always trusted me, until today, and I wish I knew why she doesn't trust me with this one thing—this one major thing. There are bigger problems to worry about, like trying to avoid playing bumper cars with the long line of commuters facing us, but I'm so upset with her I can barely make out the lines on the road. And I can't react quickly enough to slow down in time.

Dad's hand clasps my shoulder. "Watch the road, Luce!" Dad shouts, something he's never, ever done before. That's when I know it's over.

I'd made it my entire life without giving a single thought to how I would die. In the end, though, death finds me just fine without needing any help. Instead of a cloaked figure with scythe in hand, my demise comes in the form of an electric-blue semi with a cartoon alligator grinning from the door of the truck. A citrus truck, I discover, as soon as an entire grove's worth of oranges buries our SUV. I hate oranges.

The green light had turned from yellow to red before I'd made it to the intersection. Blinded by my anger, I hadn't noticed until the truck loomed across our path.

Screams batter me from every side. From the smoking brakes as I mash them to delay the inevitable. From our vehicle as it folds in on itself like some wrong kind of origami. From my mother the instant before her life slips away. From Dad as he realizes he can't save any of us. I let myself slip away to the back of my mind.

I try to come back once. Red trickles into my eyes, thankfully blocking out the worst parts of the nightmare. Several oranges bounce in my window and across my lap, drawing my attention towards the passenger side of the car. Mom's head lolls at an impossible angle, the one eye I can see crimson and rolled toward the sky. She's gone, just like that. A whimper bubbles from my bloodied lips. "No . . ." I want to scream, I want to throw up, I want to shake her by the shoulders until her heart pulses again. But, no. Trapped in my prison of steel, crying is the only thing I can manage.

"H-h-hon . . . ney . . ." he rasps, and I can't allow myself to think about why Dad's voice is so far in front of where Mom and I are still strapped in. "Are you . . . o-. . . kay?" Buried between the airbags, he's been saved from this shattered image of the woman he'd loved so fiercely. Even in this awful, horrible, bleak moment, God granted my father mercy by sparing him that.

"Daaaad." I cry harder. My nose runs, or maybe it's more blood.

"Ohhhh, Luce." He sighs. I long to look at his face again, to burn to memory every single crinkle and whisker, but I can't make my body do what I want. He's not moving at all, and my heart nearly bursts, thinking he'd died right then with his voice so heavy with sadness and blame.

He shudders and, for the briefest moment, I hold on to the faintest flicker of hope.

"I love you," he groans. "This . . . was . . . n't . . ."

Dad stills and goes silent, and so does time. Hope. Such an awful, stupid trick.

Voices float outside the car, loud voices. Shouting.

Shut up! I want to yell to whoever is making all the noise. Can't you see he hasn't finished his sentence? This wasn't what?

No matter how hard I try to turn my head in his direction, something rigid holds me there. If I fight against it, I quickly forget everything that matters in that very moment—like what I'm trying to do and why. When I struggle one last time and I lose feeling in my whole right side, I quit trying to look at him. Dad will never give me the answer I so desperately need. No one can.

As my hope crashes around my feet, along with my life and an ungodly amount of citrus, I pull away from the light . . .

I strip away the last petal from the wilting rose I'd plucked from the trellis, leaving only a browned bit of stem. The garden is cool this evening, a nice northern breeze ruffling through the leaves. It's a nice way to spend the rest of the day before I have to lock myself away for the night. The soft perfume reminds me of my parents and of happier times, when their love could be measured in crystal dishes and pink roses. Unfortunately, the good memories always bleed away to the worst memories of all. Especially here.

"And that's how I found myself in Mitte. Sorry you asked?"

Oliver doesn't answer me right away, his dark eyes focused on the wasted flowers littering the earth beneath our feet. I've never told the story before, mainly because no one who cared to hear it is still alive. Anyone else who knew me from before treated me as if I died anyway, even before the accident. My lip quivers, and I turn away from him, pretending to notice another shriveling bloom.

He moves close behind me, and I sense his hesitation to touch me because we're like magnets pushing apart and pulling together. The last thing I want is for him to care about pathetic, broken me. I've done nothing to deserve his concern. Still, my soul reaches for his, drawing him in. If he keeps his distance, hovering just out of reach, I'm afraid I'll go out of my mind with this need. Ghosts, or whatever they like to be called, shouldn't make me feel this way. It doesn't make any sense. None of this makes any sense.

"Oh, Lucy." He breathes as his fingers trace my upper arm and leave a trail of goosebumps. "I'm so sorry for everything."

I'm sorry. Anyone who has lost someone near to their heart knows "I'm sorry" is the emptiest of all human phrases, something to say when there's nothing else to say. From Oliver, who knows what it's like to lose it all, I expected a lot more. And what he says next does not disappoint.

"This wasn't your fault."

My breath catches in my throat.

Chapter 16

Within my veins, my blood turns to ice. I whirl around. "What did you just say?"

The corners of his mouth turn downward as he shuffles backward a step, taking a cue from the pain flashing in my eyes. "This . . . wasn't your fault."

When he repeats it, the hesitation causes the memory to echo even louder in my ears. Dad's words coming from Oliver's lips feel almost like a betrayal, and yet, the most bittersweet passage of poetry ever spoken. My heart throbs to the point where it hurts to fill my lungs, the pressure unbearable. The tears that fell over and over during my recollection of the crash blur again in my vision as I whisper, "How did you know that?"

"I knew, that's all." He shrugs, like it's nothing. Like he hadn't finished a dead man's sentence. Though he acts casual, his voice is gentle. It's clear that he wants very much to comfort me in some way, but he doesn't know how. I'm not sure I'd let him anyway.

I've been through so much in the past day that I've stopped reacting the way I ought to—including developing a crush on Oliver. Having feelings for him is at the very top of my not-to-do list, or it should be. No dating the dead—it sounds like a given. But when he looks at me with such intensity, like he'd throw himself in front of a moving vehicle or take on a thousand Conductors to keep me safe, it stirs up the swirl of confusion all over again.

Angry mobs surrounding me, Duke getting hurt, stumbling into The Divide, The Conductors nearly dragging me to who-knows-where, reliving the worst moments of my life before Mitte, and finding any kind of emotional energy for puppy love? Whatever. Even I can admit when I'm completely losing it. I laugh and shake my head at my own ridiculousness.

Oliver tries to keep up with the wide sway of my mood swings, but he has to blink a few times before he realizes I'm laughing instead of crying. "Are you okay?"

My laughter breaks down into shoulder-shaking rumbles and I can barely breathe. Tears stream down my face, but this time they're not from sadness. I'm seriously cracking up. Somehow I manage to gasp, "I need to go back home."

"That's fine. We should head back to the cabin soon, anyway—before sunset."

"No. I want to go back to my aunt's." Actually, I don't know what I want. Getting far, far away from Mitte sounds pretty darn appealing. But if that isn't an option—and I know it isn't—at least I can sort things out in my head a little better in my own room. There's the added benefit of not getting dragged away by Conductors if I get up in the middle of the night to pee. Yes, the more I think about indoor plumbing and electricity, the more I'm convinced that I need to return to the mansion.

Oliver doesn't share my enthusiasm for the idea. "I don't know, Lucy. I haven't talked to anyone in town to see if it's even safe to bring you out of hiding."

"I'll stay inside all night, promise." A couple days ago, his protective streak would have made me angry, but Angus hadn't confronted me and split Duke's head open on the pavement then. I shudder remembering the way Duke's head had sounded like a ripe watermelon thudding against the ground. That should have been my head split open on the pavement, and, given the right opportunity, I doubt Angus will spare me again. Now I can see what Oliver's been trying to shield me from. Danger really is all around me.

"Well . . . If you promise to stay inside, maybe," he says, stroking his chin as he stares off into the distance. "And I can stick around the orchard."

"Fine. Perfect. Let's do that," I say, impatient to get back to the house before he talks himself out of allowing it. The longer I let him think about it, the more opportunity he has to come up with a list of reasons why it's such a horrible idea. I even walk over to Jasper and swing myself into the saddle before Oliver can react.

"Hey!" He clicks his tongue behind his teeth as he approaches me. "You got lucky this time, but you might want to check to make sure the girth's tight before you get on, unless you like eating dirt." He sets his jaw in determination as he tightens the leather around Jasper's belly. It's something so routine to Oliver, and I'm sure he can do it with his eyes closed, but I have no idea what he's talking about. "I loosen the saddle so he can relax while I work," Oliver explains.

In that moment, I know the kind of man Oliver had been when he was alive. Caring and compassionate, a protector. If I'd met him at Manny's party, I'm sure he wouldn't have tried to stick his tongue in my ear uninvited and in front of half the school. He'd taken care of his family until the very end, until tragedy stole that from him. Death had tried to steal the best parts of the man standing before me, but it hadn't succeeded. If anything, his loyalty had intensified, like it was the only thing left.

Sitting behind me on the spotted horse, Oliver shows me the way back to Aunt Perdita's place, a short ride through the apple trees. All the way, his eyes scan the deepening shadows for any dangers lurking there. I let him, and I don't even roll my eyes because, even as annoying as it is, I know he can't help but protect me. Why he wants to keep me so safe when I treat him poorly and mope around, I don't have a clue, but my irritation with him slowly turns into gratefulness. Without Oliver, I would have died, or worse, several times over. Though I'm not afraid of death, necessarily, because it would mean being reunited with Mom and Dad, I don't care to die at the hands of a snarling ghost biker or creatures so awful that words fail to adequately describe them. When I choose to move on—really move on—I hope it will be on my terms and nothing more sinister than that.

The great white mansion slumbers as we enter through the French doors off the patio. I expect Aunt Perdita to meet us in a rage, hair flying out like a banshee, spewing split pea soup from her terrible mouth. Or perhaps she sits waiting in one of the stiff chairs in the parlor, hands folded in her lap, ready to interrogate and carry out a harsh sentence. I imagine her locking me away in my room for the rest of eternity, only allowing me stale heels of bread and glasses of warm water in a dented tin cup. She'll install one of those peepholes in my bedroom door so she can slide it open just wide enough for me to see her icy eyes and then snap it closed again when she finishes tormenting me. I watch too many movies.

As we slip through the shadows stretching across the parlor and into the entryway, Aunt Perdita is nowhere to be found. It doesn't surprise me, really, despite my dramatic imagination. Still, I try to quiet my awkward gait as we make our way down the corridor to my room. Oliver peeks into every unlocked room along our path, looking for any indication something is off. His search concludes at my room, where he spends a long while circling around, peering under my bed and in my closet, then in my bathroom and behind the shower door.

"Everything looks fine," he announces. He manages to sound sad and relieved, all at the same time.

I move toward the bathroom, anxious to turn on the shower and wash away the worst parts of the past day. I pause at the door, and turn to smile at him one last time before he leaves me. "I guess so. Thanks."

He hesitates near the foot of the canopy bed, running his fingers lightly across the spread. I wait for him to work out what he wants to say. When he finally speaks, all he manages is, "I'll be out in the trees, if you need me."

"Okay," I answer simply, punctuating it with a quick nod. My heart dips in my chest in disappointment at his practical statement. It's not the response I expected—from him or from me. I don't understand it, and I don't want to—at least not now. All I want is to get cleaned up and pass out in my bed, free from any more danger for the moment. Anything else is icing on the cake.

"So this is goodnight, then."

"Goodnight."

Our eyes meet, and he holds me there in an embrace. Not an actual embrace, full of tangled limbs and thrumming pulses, but something else that makes me feel strangely exposed. He doesn't dare cross the space between us to tuck me securely in his arms, but his soul reaches out for mine—just for a second. Just until heat washes over my body. Suddenly very aware of our connection, I twirl the long tail of my head scarf between my fingers and glance toward the window.

Beyond the feeble cover of the gauzy curtain, the blood-red sun stains the horizon outside.

Night follows closely on the heels of the day's fading beauty, eager to conceal every trace of her existence. Oliver needs to go to the night, too.

"It's almost—" As I turn my attention back to him, my eyes stop at the bedside table. A fresh bloom floats within the curve of the delicate bowl. My heart stops, stutters, then rushes forward in frantic motion.

Oliver knows my father's dying words, the same words Dad had been unable to complete. He knows about the pink rose my parents exchanged every week. How can he know those things? He can't, unless . . .

Unless Dad is here. In Mitte. With me. My chest swells with the idea, and tears slip down my cheeks. My father, here with me again in this awful place, makes me happy beyond words. Now I won't be alone.

But you're not alone.

I push aside my inner voice because, obviously, my inner voice can't appreciate how huge this really is. It's huger than huge.

But, Oliver . . .

Oliver. Of course! Oliver will know for sure.

"He's here?" I ask, my words hopeful. But when I glance back to the door, Oliver's gone.

I move as quickly as I can down the hall, trying to catch him before he disappears into the night. My voice echoes and crescendos from the walls and the high ceilings, punctuated by the urgent long and short notes from my flip-flops slapping on the tile. With each step, worry worms itself further into my brain, eating away at my resolve. He probably defies all laws of physics or whatever when I'm not around. He's probably halfway across the orchard by now, and I've barely made it to the parlor. My questions will have to wait for the morning.

No! I refuse to rest until I see Dad and feel him with my own hands. I need to see him whole again and warm to the touch. A spark flickers and glows beneath my skin, and I fan it forward into a blaze as I cross the foyer to the only other person who can give me the answers I seek.

My hand hovers over Aunt Perdita's door, ready to knock.

Chapter 17

I knock twice, hard, feeling bold in my search for information about my dad.

There's no answer.

I try once more, pounding a little harder. Again, silence wraps around me.

The next time I knock, I pair it with an "Aunt Perdita!" I repeat this a few more times with no response, until it's clear she's not going to open the door. My shoulders droop, and I turn back to my room.

That's when I hear it—a faint scraping on the other side of the heavy door. White-hot anger flashes through my body, momentarily blinding me. She's in there, all right. I'm not usually filled with rage, and I'm not very strong, but it doesn't stop me from wishing I could splinter her door into a million pieces just to see the look of shock on her face. The way she treats me feels wrong on so many levels, considering I've never done a thing to her, besides . . . kill her sister.

No wonder she despises the very sight of me. If the roles were reversed, maybe I'd hate me, too. No need to go to all the trouble to convince me I'm horrible for what I did. I'm already not my biggest fan.

I almost give up right then and there, defeated, until I remember why I came to my aunt in the first place. My dad's out there somewhere, and maybe just as lost and scared as I am. With renewed urgency, I pound on the door once more. "Please let me in. I need to talk to you." My voice quakes, matching the zigzag of emotions darting through me.

Silence.

Aunt Perdita's obviously in there—why won't she answer?

I bite my lower lip, dreading what surely will come next. Bursting into the room uninvited won't make friendship with my aunt any easier, nor will unanswered questions about my dad's whereabouts make it possible for me to concentrate on anything else. One more deep breath in, and I place my hand on the door handle. A breath out, and I press the handle down, simultaneously easing the door open.

The room glows harshly, and I blink furiously for several seconds until my vision gets with the program. As soon as my pupils adjust, I promptly throw up on the floor, barely missing my own feet.

"Get out of here, now!" Aunt Perdita roars, her head flying up from where it had been resting on the bed. Her bloodshot eyes protrude from her chalky, bloated face.

I stumble backward a step, trying to make sense of the scene before me. A wave of nausea hits me again, my mouth pooling with bitter saliva. My body becomes sticky with sweat. The tangy metallic smell of blood and something burning does me no favors, and I heave again, this time finding a wastebasket near the doorway.

Doc Blevins, dressed in gore-stained surgical scrubs, crouches over her wide-open abdomen, wielding a razor-sharp scalpel that glitters dangerously in the lights. He's gutting her alive, with no anesthesia, no hospital room, no witnesses . . . except me.

"What's . . ." I take a woozy step forward, sure that I need to save her from this madman. The room spins around me and I pause.

The doctor shoots Aunt Perdita an anxious look, which is when I notice the circular mass of dark, coagulated blood at the base of his spine.

"You—you've been shot?" I choke after heaving over the wastebasket again.

"I TOLD YOU TO GET OUT," my aunt shrieks.

It's an image I'll remember for the rest of my life—or the rest of whatever this is. No matter how much she despises me, I don't want any harm to come to her. My definition of harm definitely includes being dissected while still alive, with her vital organs arranged on the sheet next to her like they're playing a real, live game of Operation. And she's demanding I leave her here to this torture.

Tears flood my eyes, and I stagger toward the door. "I'm so sorry. So, so, sorry." Sobs wrack my body as I back into the doorjamb. I can't remember why I came here in the first place, but I know I'd been desperate for her help. Now I feel sick, drowning in sadness as I watch the life drain from my only remaining family.

Alone, once again. Everything else fades into the background.

My aunt turns her face from me, focusing instead on the blank wall. With a sober expression, Doc's eyes meet mine. "Lucy, please leave us. You can't help her, as much as I know you want to."

I manage the smallest of nods, letting the truth of his words sink in. That horrible, glaring white room will become her tomb, I know without a doubt. I leave her to the doctor's mercy because I know I cannot save them. I can't save anyone at all, not even myself. No, I was born to destroy.

The moonlight washes through the great wall of windows as I thud through the parlor. He said he would be in the orchard if I needed him, and I'm pretty sure this counts as a need. The night had flown in to nest for the evening, a black raven with wings of violet blue. The full moon floats high above, cutting a smoky path through the void. I can make out my steps easily, guided by the faint light above, but still I move with slow, deliberate steps. My skin crawls over my frame, wanting to be anywhere else but out in the open where God-only-knows-what can easily spot me.

Hurry, hurry, hurry!

This time I agree with my inner voice, cursing my hip as it clicks and sticks, biting my tongue raw each time my undependable ankle protests beneath my weight. The welcoming arms of the trees urge me forward, and I train my eyes on the goal. Only in the shelter of the trees will I stop to call out for Oliver. I don't know why, but the trees seem like good secret-keepers. They won't turn me over to the darkness. It's true that they're trees, without the ability to discern right from wrong or good from evil, which is lucky for me since I can't quite figure out which side I belong to.

Finally, I reach the deepest shadows of the orchard, and I collapse against the trunk of the nearest tree. Then and only then do I allow myself to think again about the grisly things happening back at the mansion. As soon as her tortured face forms in my mind, I have to think of something else. My stomach rolls, though there's nothing left to lose.

You shouldn't be out here. Focus!

I nod in agreement. Though it's dark, I close my eyes to shut out the grey forms swaying at the edge of the grove. The orchard appears smaller than it had last time I ventured here after dark. Then, it seemed to stretch on and on endlessly. The gentle breeze trails across my bare skin, and I hope it will deliver my message to Oliver alone. But what if he isn't the one to hear my plea—I haven't thought this through very well, or at all.

What option do I have? Stay here and wait for The Conductors to put me out of my misery? Or return to the house where I'll be haunted by what I witnessed tonight? I utter a prayer under my breath, asking for God to help, though I'm not sure if He can hear anyone in this forsaken place.

Now. Call out to him now.

"I need you, Oliver." The words come as naturally as an exhale, barely louder than a whisper. The desperation in my words push them deep into the gloom. I don't know how I'll know if he heard me, or how long to wait, but it's not long at all before I pick up the sound of heavy footfalls traveling my direction. To be safe, I hold my breath and curl into a ball near the base of the nearest tree. Hiding is probably a waste of time, as

I'm probably the only person in this town who can't see in the dark. Funny—even in a town full of strange things, I'm still the freak.

"Lucy," he breathes into the night, so very close.

Relief floods over me at the sound of his voice and his nearness. I clamber to my feet and turn in a slow circle, trying to place him within the darkness. Before I can make out his outline against that of the trees, Oliver finds me. His hand moves up to stroke my cheek tenderly, hesitating when he feels the traces of my tears.

"What is it?" His hushed voice brims with concern.

I can't answer him because I've broken down crying again. I throw my arms around his neck to support myself, and bury my face in his chest. He stiffens beneath me, caught off guard by my embrace. After a moment, he softens and wraps his arms around me, resting his chin against the top of my head. It's the safest I've felt in a very long time, and I don't want it to end even though I know the longer we stay here the greater our chances of discovery. There's already been enough discovery for one day. My body shudders, living and reliving my aunt's butchering, and I nuzzle closer to him.

He slides one hand up and down my back, firmly but gently. "*Shh, shh.* Lucy, tell me what's wrong."

"My . . . my aunt." I hiccup. "She's dead."

"Of course she is. I thought you knew."

I shake my head against his chest. "No! I mean, yes." This isn't coming out right, so I start over. "Yes— I guess I knew she was gone, or else she wouldn't be here, right? But I saw her. Tonight. He had cut her stomach open and . . ."

At my words, Oliver's grip on me loosens. I press my body against him harder to make up for it.

"This isn't the way I wanted you to find out," he sighs.

I don't like the sound of that, and I pull back enough to look him in the eye, an impossibility in the dark. "Find out what?"

Oliver untangles himself from our embrace, even though I try to hold on. Whatever's about to happen isn't going to make me feel any better. Oliver confirms the bad feeling when he says, "Remember, I'm still me. Please, Lucy."

Words fly far away from me as I watch him take the handful of steps until he's no longer shielded by the boughs of the apple trees. I want to stop him before he commits to that last step, to convince him I'm okay not knowing. But I don't call to him, and he only pauses for a moment before he bows his head and takes one big step back into the clearing.

The bright moonlight washes over his body, illuminating every piece death had claimed for its own.

195

Chapter 18

"No," I moan, covering my mouth with my hands. "No, no. I can't look—"

Sorrow fills his blackened eyes at my reaction. A trickle of blood, glistening in the faint light, streams from his forehead and another from the corner of his mouth. There are a host of other injuries, I'm sure, but I can't bear to see them.

"I don't unders—"

He holds up a hand, indicating I should quiet myself. I freeze, listening for unknown rustling off in the distance, but hear nothing. Just in case, I shrink back against the tree. If the thing doesn't see me, my heart shaking every inch of my body will totally give me away.

Oliver glides to me and takes me in his arms again. My body tenses against his.

"Remember, I'm still me," he breathes into my ear. "And I'll explain later, but right now I need you to get back into the house."

"But Aunt Perdita's in there. It's so awful."

He squeezes me. "I know, but The Conductors are patrolling. I can't risk you getting caught."

My stomach turns at the thought of stepping back into the house alone. Before tonight, I felt safe enough there, even if my aunt had been a less-than-welcoming hostess. Now the cool halls and monochrome hues chill me to the bone.

"Please, Lucy! You've got to go now," he pleads. "I'll go with you."

We make our way through the clearing as quickly as we can, with me leaning on him. Each step closer to the house multiplies my feeling of dread, but there really isn't another choice. Not one where I don't have a personal escort into the pits of Hell, at least.

Only once I'm safely inside the parlor can Oliver relax. I wish I could relax, too, but the house frightens me about as much as the reeking demonic police officers. Oliver believes I'll be okay here, but I don't share his rosy outlook on the situation. I've traded the weight of worry of being discovered outdoors for straight-up fear of absolutely everything.

I stand just inside the door, leaving it cracked a few inches so I can still have some sort of contact with the only thing in my life keeping me sane. I try to convince him not to leave me alone, to come inside and keep me company since it's not very likely I'll sleep. He, of course, tells me it's against his rules, but he refuses to tell me what that means.

"Go to sleep, Luce," he says simply, the corners of his mouth tugging upward. "I'll be here in the morning."

"Go to sleep? You've got to be kidding me," I huff. "I'll probably never sleep again. But, thanks. Now you go ahead and have fun on your scavenger hunt or whatever."

He chuckles, though I'm not trying to be funny. "First thing tomorrow morning I'll come by. Until then . . ." Oliver opens the door wide enough to pull me back to his chest. Light as a feather, he brushes his lips against the top of my head where my scarf covers my own reminders of life's frailty, the system of pink, puffy scars. The beating of my heart jolts into a syncopated rhythm, tired from trying to keep up with all the highs and lows.

I don't know what to say to his unexpected bit of PDA. My brain temporarily loses track of things like words and how to make them come out of my mouth, so I don't say anything at all. I feel my face turn crimson, and I thank my lucky stars for the cover of darkness.

I wait at the doors and watch him slip back into the trees before I head back to my room. The only way to make it through the rest of the night alone is to pretend like none of this happened. While I peel off my tank top and shorts, I pretend that Aunt Perdita is tucked away in her room, sipping tea and reading a smutty romance novel. As I fill the bathtub with warm water and bubbles, I imagine Oliver and Jasper out enjoying a nice moonlit ride around the countryside. I close my eyes and sink below the surface of the water, trying to wash away reality with lavender bubble bath. None of those troubling things actually happened. It was all a bad dream. A really bad dream.

I'd almost convinced myself when something catches my eye from across the room. My scarf hangs from the bathroom doorknob. Dark stains mar the delicate fabric. His kiss. His blood.

Eventually the water cools and I force myself out of the tub. In the seclusion of the bathroom, the air thick with steam, it had been easier to shut out the nightmares. Out in my room, the barely-covered windows expose me to any horrors lurking nearby. Common sense tells me I would be harder to spot with the lights off, but common sense doesn't offer any good advice for how to sit in a dark room alone after what I've seen.

I spend most of the night with the lights blazing, huddled in a ball at the head of the bed. I try and fail to keep my mind full of happy things, boring things, *anything* to keep the knot of fear from overtaking me. How long I sit there until I end up dozing off, I'm not sure. One moment I occupy my brain with working out a made-up algebra problem, the most mundane and useless thing I can come up with, the next I wake up bathed in sunlight, sprawled across my bed.

"Good morning, sunshine," a deep voice greets me from the corner of the room.

The voice, the first I've heard since leaving Oliver in the darkness, causes me to yelp and scramble upright into a feral crouch. So stupid of me to let my guard down! I blink furiously, trying to focus my eyes and locate the intruder. My chest heaves in and out in anger and determination to survive.

"Sorry." Oliver puts his hands up to try to calm me down. "I didn't mean to startle you."

Oh, Oliver.

Oliver!

Besides looking wearier than I've ever seen him, he is himself—no blood oozing from any orifice and no bruised eyes. Relieved, I bound off the mattress and into his arms. A grin sweeps over his face as he pulls me closer, and he returns to being the boy I know and find myself starting to care for. I close my eyes and relax against his chest while my heart rate calms to a more conservative pace. Something about being near to him, touching him, makes me feel like everything's going to turn out okay, a tall order for my current situation. Maybe it won't all be okay, but I breathe him in and breathe him out instead of thinking about what comes next. For now, it is okay.

"Lucy, you are so unexpected," he whispers. "So amazingly unexpected." His hand travels upward along my spine, igniting sparks of sensation in its path. I shiver and hold my breath as his fingers trace the back of my neck and come to rest at the back my head.

He tucks his chin to look down at me. There's something like wonder in his earthen eyes, something I can't understand. I've done nothing to deserve his wonder or even his attention. Still, his hand carefully angles my head so our eyes can meet. It's hard to deny his feelings when I see them reflected back to me. Overwhelmed, I shut my eyes and pull a shaky breath in through my lips to steady my shrieking nerves. Oliver leans down lower and I can feel him close to my lips. His callused fingers slip across the fragile skin lining my scalp, and I gasp.

My head! I push away from him with both hands, frantic to break our connection.

What are you doing? No! No, you don't! Not right now. You're not worried about the stupid scarf, are you?

Oh, you know, the scarf and that whole thing about him being dead. I mean, I'll admit I'm not normal and I've quite possibly lost my mind, but, seriously. Kissing a guy who was dripping blood from his mouth like a zombie a few hours ago? What was I thinking? That can't happen.

He stares at me, stunned, his mouth hanging open. I snatch a clean scarf from my dresser drawer and escape to the bathroom. Once I've wrapped the scarf around my head, fortifying my defenses once more, I take a deep breath to calm myself.

The shimmer of the sun through the bowl on my bedside table flickers in my eyes when I come back out of the bathroom. I'd forgotten all about it, as it seemed pretty insignificant in light of Aunt Perdita's . . . situation. But it floods back to me now, every unanswered question and every sliver of hope. Oliver follows my longing gaze to the rose, and then snaps back to look at my face.

"That rose," I point toward the bowl, "was here last night when you left me. Did you leave it?"

He doesn't answer, but looks toward the window instead.

"I mean, you and I were together all day, so I don't know when you would've had the time."

"Maybe I left it overnight while you were sleeping at my house."

"Did you really? Did you come into this house *at night*, breaking the rules, to leave this flower for me?" I place my hands on my hips and raise an eyebrow.

Oliver studies my expression for a minute, setting his jaw. "No."

"Then who did?"

He refuses to answer me.

"Come on," he says, motioning toward the hallway.

I want to grab him by the shoulders and shake until the answer spills from his lips, but I know Oliver won't tell me anything until he's good and ready. I sigh and follow him.

When we reach the front door, I pause before I open it. It had been a long, warm day yesterday and today won't be much different. "I'm going to grab some water from the kitchen. Want some?"

Oliver shakes his head, but something more flashes in his expression. He's probably just being polite by not asking me for food. I write it off as a pride thing, probably something connected to his generation that had been tossed to the wayside.

I round the corner into the kitchen. Oliver's close behind, and slams into my back when I stop without warning. There, huddled over the island, is Aunt Perdita. Other than looking a little bit groggy as she eyes me over the lip of her coffee mug, she doesn't look like someone who had just been murdered by the kindly old country doctor.

"But you're—" I start, shocked.

Grabbing my elbow and taking charge, Oliver spins me around and rushes both of us from the kitchen.

"But she was—" I can't form the words; all I can do is stutter and glance over my shoulder as he steers me out the front door.

"I know, I know," he coos, placing his hands on my trembling shoulders. "Listen to me very carefully. You're not crazy."

I don't believe him, do you? We feel kind of crazy.

"Are you okay?"

I pull in a deep breath and give him a quick nod. "I guess."

He slides his hands into his pockets and looks out over the front yard. Norman glances up at us from the flowerbed he's weeding. Oliver tilts his head in greeting to his friend, then sighs. "Well, Lucy. It's time you knew."

I stare at him, suddenly afraid of what he's about to say. Very quietly, I manage, "He was killing her. She was dying. I don't understand."

"This is the curse, I guess you could say. We're stuck in this place, day after day, remembering the things we wish we could have done differently in our own lives. During the day, we're whole, but every night we must relive our death. The night breaks us all—there's no rest from it." His face is haunted. "'Cept for you. That's how I knew you weren't dead. You don't change at night, and you sleep. Better than that, you *dream*."

"How do you know I dream?"

Red blotches appear on his cheeks and he looks away. "Because I watched you when you were sleeping—at my house and then this morning. You talk in your sleep, too."

It's my turn to blush. "No, I don't." I laugh and swat at his arm. "What do I say?"

"That I'm the man of your dreams, of course." He flashes a crooked smile my way.

"Quit changing the subject, Oliver. I need to know about Mitte."

He presses his lips together, his smile fading. "All right. How much time you got?"

I bring my hand up to block the morning sun. The world around me stands quiet and unmoving, nothing changing, as if time has simply stopped. Even Norman's motionless among the flowers, watching us with fearful eyes. Maybe it's just me, but I'm beginning to sense a theme here.

I let my hand drop to my side and blow out a heavy breath. "Forever, I guess."

Chapter 19

Against Oliver's better judgment, I convince him to talk with me as we walk down the quiet street. He's nervous the others will spot me and do to me what they did to Duke. Naturally, I'm afraid of that, too, but I don't have a whole lot to lose. Being pretty much half-dead anyway has its advantages, I guess.

Oliver tells me again about Mitte acting as a dumping ground, of sorts, for spirits who have passed on. "Each one of us is here for a reason—something we never did that we wanted to. Some of us are here 'cause we failed to do something."

I take a few slow steps, studying the pavement, before I ask, "Well, which is it?"

He blinks. "What?"

"Why are you here?"

He pulls his mouth into a thin line, his cue to me that he's not ready to talk about it. His silence is pretty annoying after spilling all of the details of the crash, but whatever. I've never personally died, so maybe it's harder to talk about than nearly dying. Or maybe he's just being Oliver again, frustrating and . . . frustrating.

I decide to take the pressure off. "So, what about my aunt? My parents never said much about her, so I don't know how she passed."

"Most of us don't ask or want to know. It's enough having to think about your own death every day for the rest of time without having to think about other people's, too. But I know about Miss Perdita."

My pulse picks up in my veins. I'm not sure if I really want to know now that I'm on the brink of finding out. "Yeah?"

"She died during childbirth. I'm told they—" He shudders. "—cut her baby out. I don't know too much about that."

"A C-section?"

He shrugs. "Like I said, I don't know about babies. All's I know is she didn't survive, and here she is."

I let this info roll around in my head, lining it up with what I'd witnessed in my aunt's room last night. "And Doc? He was her surgeon?"

Oliver shakes his head. "No, but Doc just happens to be Mitte's only doctor. When he showed up, the two of them kinda paired up to kill two birds with one stone, guess you could say." He kicks a pebble with the toe of his boot, sending it skittering down the road. "Dying's better with someone else."

"Doc," I say. "His head was bleeding."

"I know about Doc, too, but don't tell him I told you because he's mighty ashamed of it."

"Who am I going to tell?"

"True." Oliver glances down the street before he continues. "Well, Doc cheated on his wife with one of his nurses. When the missus found out, she walked into the hospital and shot him in the back of the head," Oliver says, and my mouth drops open. When he sees the shocked look on my face, he backpedals. "Listen, Luce. He was a good man—still is—and feels awful for what he did."

I bury my face in my hands and groan. How much of this can I take before the sadness pulls me under?

Along the way, a fat orange cat darts out in front of us from the refuge of the underbody of a rusted-out Cadillac. My heart practically leaps into my throat, and I press my hand to my chest to make sure it's still *lub-dubbing* away.

"And the cats. Why are there only cats and no other animals?"

"Because they're cats."

When I blink at him, unsure of his meaning, he laughs. "Don't tell me you don't know about cats."

"Nope. My dad is—was—allergic. He'd break out in hives if a cat even looked at him."

"People with cats understand that those dang felines rule the world." He grins, looking after the cat, who now sits proudly on the sidewalk, watching us through narrowed eyes. "Guess it's kind of true, because they're all over the place. Maybe it's that whole 'nine lives' thing. But you're forgetting about Jasper."

"Jasper's practically a person, though."

Oliver's smile is bittersweet as he looks back at the horse. Jasper wanders behind us, snatching occasional mouthfuls of grass from the side of the road. "You're right about that. That horse is far better than a person, most days."

I smile at Oliver's obvious fondness for his opinionated companion. "So, let me get this straight—Jasper's here because he has some kind of unfinished business?"

Oliver shrugs. "You'd have to ask him for yourself."

That response is just what I've come to expect from him: frustrating. I blow out a puff of air. Still, I steal a glance at the big brown and white horse, who raises his head and pricks his ears in our direction.

Well, would it be the weirdest thing about this place if the horse actually talked?

Good point.

We continue down the street, passing the rows of houses and the assortment of vehicles parked in the driveways or by the curbs. "I know this is silly, but another thing I've been wondering is about all of the cars. I mean, there's one in front of, like, every house. I've never seen one move the whole time I've been in Mitte, unless you count the taxi that brought me here."

Oliver scratches his chin. "The taxi—now that's a little interesting because we aren't supposed to make really big things happen, like moving a car from its parking spot. The living notice that."

My eyes widen. "The living? You mean there are live people here?" I scan the neighborhood for any sign that I'm not the only one. I'm not sure how to tell them apart from the dead since everyone here looks as alive as, if not more alive than, I do.

"Not really. The best I can figure, our world is sort of a reflection of some place that exists among the living. We all bring pieces of our humanity with us here—like my family's cabin or maybe even Bud's taxi. Other than that, most of Mitte doesn't belong to us. We're spooks, you know. Ghosts.

"Bud never came out and said it, but I heard from somewhere that he fell asleep at the wheel with paying customers riding along. Drove right off a bridge." Oliver moves his hand in a line and then arcs it until he slaps his hands together to signify impact.

At least you're not the only bad driver to set foot in this town.

I shake my head to clear my disturbing inner thought. "What happened to not wanting to know everyone's story?"

"That's where you heard me wrong. I said most of us don't want to know," he points out. "I like to meet people, get to know them, find out if they'll make this place more pleasant or more difficult."

"What's your verdict on me?" I ask, my eyes sparkling.

"So far, I'd say a little bit of both." He smirks.

Pretending to be offended, I yelp and smack him in the arm. He laughs, genuinely laughs, and swerves out of my reach in case I decide to swat him again. His laughter plays like a melody in my ears, and I wish I knew the secret to making it happen more often. There isn't a whole lot to be thrilled about in Mitte, and just his little bit of happiness makes everything more bearable.

Too soon our smiles fade, and I make one last observation. "Life, or whatever this is, seems to go on. Everyone's eating at the diner, my aunt has her morning cup of joe, you prune roses. It seems so ordinary. I don't get it."

"We're creatures of habit, Luce, all of us—even you. It only gets worse on the other side. Our routines are the only thing we have left to remind us that, once, there used to be more than—" He sweeps his arm out toward the ghost town. "—just this."

Oliver says it'll be okay to stop by the orphanage since I've been worried about how Duke was healing up after Angus' attack. I knock on the front door and wait, then knock again. No answer.

"They're probably in town," Oliver says.

I raise my eyebrows in silent question, my eyes flitting toward the center of Mitte.

"It's a really bad idea, Lucy."

"Please, Oliver?" I clasp my hands together under my chin and flutter my lashes. I'm not above using what little feminine charm I possess to sway him. If that doesn't work, I'll resort to flat-out begging.

Oliver stares at me, his expression rigid, until he drops his shoulders with a heavy sigh. "Fine," he says. "But if I see anything—or anyone—suspicious, we're out of there."

We'd traveled a couple blocks when I hear scuffling coming from an alley off to our right. The old, bent-over woman I saw meandering down the street the other day in her housecoat and tattered pink slippers is there, pacing. She must wander around aimlessly a lot because Oliver doesn't even seem to notice she's there. Her mouth moves in noiseless conversation as she wrings her gnarled hands, then she turns her back to us and shuffles away.

I catch Oliver by the wrist, and he looks down at my hand on his skin. There's no time for that. "She looks like she needs help."

"Sadie needs more help than most of us. She's not in her right mind."

The woman creaks in our direction again. Her eyes swim with confusion. She reminds me of my Nonna when she finally had to be put in a nursing home. I'm pretty sure Sadie has Alzheimer's, or something close.

I squeeze Oliver's wrist. "Give me a second, okay?"

He nods.

"Sadie, can you hear me?" I call as I head toward the old lady. The last thing I want is to startle her.

"Don't bother. I don't think she remembers her own name, Lucy."

I shoot him a dirty look over my shoulder. "Shush! She can hear you."

He puts his hands up, and I focus back on Sadie, who had tottered up to the side of one of the homes near the alley. She peers through one of the windows, cupping a crooked hand over her eyes. Not satisfied with what she sees through the glass, she returns to her pacing and hand-wringing. Since she won't respond to me or even so much look in my direction, I place myself directly in her path.

"How did she go?" I mouth to Oliver, afraid to upset Sadie any further.

"Old age, in a place where there were a lot of other older people who also needed help."

A home.

Sadie won't meet my eyes when I grasp her by her jutting shoulders. I don't mind—I don't need her to look at me, just as long as she listens. "Sadie, I need you to hear me." Her eyes stare past me and down at the ground. "Can you hear me?" No change.

"I told you, she's—" Oliver starts. I glare at him and he shuts his mouth.

Images of my own fragile grandmother overwhelm me when I close my eyes to gather my thoughts. The illness had stolen away so many things that made Nonna, Nonna, including, but not limited to, her fiery spirit and her kick-butt chimichangas. I want to break down in the middle of the road and cry for my grandmother, but I clench my jaw and swallow the lump in my throat.

This isn't about Nonna, not really, but I've always wished I had the chance to tell her what I'm about to share with Sadie. I only hope that what I tell her is the right thing.

"Grandma, can you hear me?" I ask, craning my neck to try to place my face in her line of sight. "Grandma, please listen."

I've about given up when her eyes rotate toward mine and pool with tears.

"Sarah. Is that really you?" She squints to see better, and a teardrop slides down the cracks of her worn face.

I falter, unsure of how to answer, then smile back at her. "Yes, it's me, Grandma. Sarah."

You're probably not doing yourself any favors by lying in Purgatory.

Jesus Himself wouldn't be able to look this poor woman in the face and say any differently.

That's probably true. Carry on, Sarah.

"Oh, thank Heavens it's you." Her voice trembles with emotion. Behind me, Oliver gasps, but I'm too afraid to look away from Sadie and risk losing her forever.

"Grandma, I've missed you so much." My lower lip begins to quiver.

She reaches up with her wrinkled hand and cradles my cheek in her palm. "Me too, child. I'm so sorry if I've been a burden to you."

Tears fall from my eyes and trail onto her skin. "Never, Grandma. You've never been a burden to any of us, and you never will be. I love you."

Sadie's thin lips split into a warm, toothless smile, the last expression she wears before she disappears.

Before I crumple to the ground, overtaken by my own sadness, Oliver catches me in his arms.

"I know why you're here," he breathes.

Chapter 20

Letty comes out of nowhere, or maybe it only seems that way because I'm still blinking away the tears for Sadie . . . and my Nonna. I'd been so lost in the moment that a marching band could have snuck up on me.

The wiry woman grabs both of my hands in hers. Her whole body flutters, and her eyes have grown to about three sizes larger than normal. "I saw that," she squeaks, glancing rapidly between me and Oliver. "What did I just see? Where did Sadie go?"

Oliver loosens his grip on me in order to rest a hand on Letty's shoulder. "We're not sure, Miss Letty. Can you keep it a secret from the others until we figure some things out?"

She ignores Oliver and leans in so she's nearly nose-to-nose with me. "Please help—"

"That's enough." Oliver's words are stern.

"—them." She finishes. The girls straggle up the sidewalk toward us. Letty pulls back from me just long enough to motion them over. Before they reach us, she drops her voice and urges, "Help them. I'm begging you."

"Lucy's been through a lot. Give her a little time to—"

"Both of you, stop it!" I cry, squeezing my eyes shut in a weak attempt to center myself. They quiet, shocked at my admonition.

I am Lucy. Only Lucy. Letty wants me—no, is *begging* me—to save them, like I have any clue how to do that. I kill, not rescue, everyone I care for. They have the wrong girl.

Magnolia reaches me first, wrapping her chubby arm around my leg in greeting. She focuses her gigantic blue eyes on me. "You didn't get any ice cream." After all was said and done, Maggie was most concerned about my lack of junk food. I laugh.

I lift my head from Oliver's chest and manage a tired smile for the others. Duke isn't with them, and panic washes over me. Oliver promised me he would be okay, but where is he? Before I can ask, I notice the bundle in Tessa's arms. Nestled in

Tessa's embrace is a baby who looks pretty fresh from the oven.

As if my faith hasn't been shaken enough already with all I've lived and all I've experienced in this place, the sight of that ruddy-cheeked little one with curious blue eyes focused on Tessa's face deals a heavy blow. It's enough for grown people to suffer unspeakable torture each night, imprisoned by their grief. But now this little one, too? It's too much.

"A baby?" I croak, more tears spilling from my eyes.

"This is Johanna," Letty says.

Maggie runs over to touch the bundle with her stubby fingers. "But I call her JoJo, 'cause her real name's too hard."

"Johanna came to us two days go," Letty explains. Her voice quiets, but each word stretches thin and tight like a rubber band on the verge of popping. "They'll keep sending them to me. It'll never end."

I can't take any more. My head needs time to sort out everything swirling in my brain. Wiping my eyes and my runny nose with the back of my hand, I turn my eyes up to Oliver. "Please, let's go."

"All right." Oliver nods, stroking the back of my head with his hand. "We're leaving now," he says to the others.

"You'll think about my request, won't you, Lucy?"

My current Plan A involves running away and thinking about as little as possible, including her big scheme to somehow transform me into a superhero. Instead, I offer a tiny nod. "I'll try. To think about it, that is."

"Leave her be, Letty." There's a hint of edge to Oliver's command. He's on guard again, and gratitude surges through me. Letty likely poses no threat to me, physically, but her tenacity could easily push my sanity past its breaking point. I know it and he knows it, and he reacts quickly.

Leaving one arm anchored around my shoulders, Oliver peers down the street and whistles. With an answering nicker, Jasper trots our way. Maggie claps and grins as the horse approaches, while Tessa's eyes grow in adoration. What is it about girls and horses, anyway? Before yesterday, I'd never understood the almost instinctual draw to the big animals—then again, I'm not really your typical girl. At this moment, though, I totally get it. Watching Jasper slide to a stop inches from Oliver's side makes me smile through my tears.

"You're driving," Oliver announces. Before I can react, he launches me into the saddle.

"Ladies." He brings two fingers to his brow in a salute. None of them responds, watching as he swings himself into place behind me.

"You watch too many movies, you know that?" I sigh as we walk away.

"Movies?"

"Movies didn't exist when you were alive? How old *are* you?"

"It was 1864 when I passed—the twenty-fourth of June. I was nineteen then. Don't really know how long it's been since then."

"Yeah, you probably don't want to know," I reply quietly.

He had been so young when he died, a young man only beginning to build his own life. My chest aches for him and what that must have been like—until I remember that I'm stuck in Mitte with him and the others, doomed to live each day as if it were my last. We ride in silence for a while as I let that horrifying tidbit sink into my brain.

My head's throbbing, the beginning of what will turn into a colossal migraine. I get them a lot, thanks to a car stuck in my cranium and the resulting surgery to remove said car. Even though I've grown used to their occurrence, I still don't know how to do life while I have one. Trying to keep my eyes open to steer Jasper sounds like a pretty awful idea, and Oliver suggests we head back to Aunt Perdita's so I can rest.

Returning to the house that had scared me so badly last night doesn't seem to be such a frightening prospect now. True, Aunt Perdita dies each night under the skilled hands of a dirty, rotten cheater, and only a matter of a handful of rooms away from mine. Now that I know she'll be alive and back to her grumpy self each morning, the house isn't as ominous. Plus, indoor plumbing. That's about as close to a win-win as I'm going to get.

Oliver tucks me into bed before heading off to find me something to eat. I tell him I can't stomach anything when my head gets like this, but he won't listen, of course, and it hurts too badly to bother arguing with him. I fall into dreamless sleep before he makes it back with a cold-cut sandwich and glass of water.

The next time I open my eyes, my migraine has downgraded itself to something more tolerable. I'm alone, which, to my surprise, disappoints me. Darkness seeps in through the thin curtains, and I draw the covers around my shoulders to ward off a chill shuddering through my body. At that very moment, Oliver is dying. At that moment, *everyone* in Mitte is dying. I roll toward my bedside table and grab one of the halves of the sandwich Oliver made me, now probably closer to a science experiment than actual food. I take a bite, staring at the rose in its glass house. If Dad was here, he would know what to do.

I wake up again to the grey light of morning. After my shower, I dress and venture down to the kitchen, waiting for Aunt Perdita to come out for her coffee. She doesn't come out of her room the whole time I dawdle at the counter, stirring my Cheerios around with a spoon until they fall apart into mush. She hasn't shown me the least bit of kindness since I stepped foot in her house, but now it kind of makes sense. Each and every person in this wretched place is miserable; some people just hide it better than others.

I don't know why I'm here. Oliver seems to think I'm here to release them all from a fate worse than death itself. To be a savior, one has to be special in some way. I've only ever been special in that I'd been able to pick up one foot and put it down quickly, rinse and repeat. I'd had a family who loved me—that had been pretty special, too. It isn't very special to take all that good away from yourself. Even knowing how broken I am, Oliver still believes I've come for a higher purpose. I still maintain that he's a wee bit dramatic.

For a few days, we pretend like nothing happened with Sadie or any of the others, and that we're just spending time together exploring the town. Oliver continues to let me sit in the saddle when we ride Jasper around, and even teaches me how to ask him for a trot once I'm balanced enough to do so. After a while, I start looking forward to our rides.

It's probably all in my head, but I even think I notice my legs getting stronger, and the limp in my one side becoming less and less. I push it away as a combination of wishful thinking and heat exhaustion.

It's turning out to be a pleasant existence, eating, sleeping, riding all day, and nearly always in the company of a certain tall, dark, and handsome gentleman. It's the stuff romance novels are written about—well, really boring romance novels written about girls with a thing for ghosts. Okay, so it's *nothing* like the stuff romance novels are written about. It would be easy for me to continue on this way forever. But, like all good stories, this one must come to an end, too.

Chapter 21

Deep down, I know my time with Oliver can't last. Somehow there will be an end, and I feel it creeping toward us like the dusk. Oliver must feel it, too, because he's barely left my side, except to die. Determined to soak up each remaining second like a sponge, tonight we spend our last moments of lingering sun lying on a blanket surrounded by nodding roses.

A wisp of clouds swirls above the canopy of trees, blown by the whisper of a breeze. The air trails across my skin, and I close my eyes, happy for the memory. When I open them again and turn my face to him, Oliver's watching me. He grins when our eyes meet.

"What?" My cheeks heat up beneath his gaze.

"I can't believe you're actually here," he whispers. "I'd hoped you'd make it, but . . ."

His words confuse me, as always, but I'm used to it now.

"I can't believe I'm here, either."

The magnitude of what might happen in the next few days rushes back into my mind, and I turn from him and stare at the sky again. "Tell me what to do, Oliver. I'm so lost right now." My voice cracks and my lips tremble.

Oliver props himself up on an elbow and leans in so he obscures my view of all else. In that moment, he's my entire world—every sight my eyes can take in, each breath in my lungs, every drop of blood within my veins—everything. I won't fight myself and the differences between us. We aren't so different, after all. He passed from life into death, and I've been brought from death into life. Destined for each other, we've met in the middle.

The breath catches in my throat as his fingers caress the line of my jaw and down the pulse of life along my throat, igniting heat beneath his touch. He slides his hand upwards, nudging away my lavender scarf until he exposes each and every visible scar. I swallow, holding his gaze as he runs his fingertips across the pink suture first, then presses his lips against my forehead. A jolt of electricity shoots through my scar, and I stiffen, waiting for pain. Instead, my head rushes with warmth.

"I love you, Lucy," he confesses, pulling back to focus those dark eyes on my reaction.

My face flares and my heart thunders in my chest. *He loves me.* Do I love him? I *want* to love him, but I'm so broken. He deserves a girl all in one piece.

Oliver doesn't wait for me to reply, closing the space between us. Though I'm undecided on my level of romantic feeling for the man in front of me, I know without a doubt I want to kiss him. My lips part slightly and I slide my eyelids closed in anticipation of his mouth on mine.

Across the garden, someone clears their throat. The spell fractures into a million pieces, Oliver lurches away from me, and I snap up to sitting. An overreaction, maybe, but we *are* the ones trying to avoid The Conductors.

"Sorry to, uh, *interrupt*," Aunt Perdita says. She's frozen in place like a deer in headlights, a pink bloom shivering in the breeze between her fingers.

The puzzle pieces *clickclickclick* together as my eyes travel a path from her shocked expression to the garden shears—*the rose!*—and back again. "What are you doing with that?" I scramble to my feet as I nod at the pink rose clutched in her hand.

Aunt Perdita blinks rapidly, glancing between me and Oliver. It's almost as if she's receiving some sort of ghostly telegram containing a better answer than the truth. "With what?" she finally says, in what can only be described as the weakest ghost telegram response ever.

She paints on a smile and turns, letting the pale bloom slip from her fingers to the earth. For as light and delicate as the flower is, it may as well have been a grand piano crashing from the tallest floor of the Empire State Building.

"No. No, no, no." I shake my head and cover my eyes with my hands. "The roses didn't come from you!"

Aunt Perdita doesn't move for what feels like an eternity, then dips her chin.

"How could you?" Blood fills my face and shoves out my words. "That wasn't yours! That wasn't your memory!"

My aunt, the traitor, avoids the fire in my glare by focusing on a tuft of clover directly in front of her designer sandals. "I'm so—"

"Stop!" I erupt like a volcano, rocketing to my feet like a plume of lava. I don't want to hear the rest. I don't want her to put into words my deepest fear: that my dad isn't here and it's been her all this time.

Oliver reaches up and wraps a hand around my elbow to keep me from launching myself at my aunt. "Miss Perdita, I reckon it'd be good for you to go."

For once, she does something right. She barely nods and turns to leave, crushing the lonely rose beneath her feet. Without a word, she glides off into the shadows.

With my mouth hanging open, I watch her disappear. I want to ask Oliver what just happened, but the words lodge somewhere between my racing brain and breaking heart. I've lost my last shred of hope, the hope that Dad would come out of hiding and we could be together again. We could never be the same, of course, but we would at least be together. But now I know that will never happen. I've held myself together for too long, but this last blow shatters me. I collapse against Oliver, who wraps his arms around me.

As I sob into his shoulder, my tears soaking through his linen shirt, something else rises in me. Not hope. Not love. Not even anger.

Determination.

I've got to end this. I've got to get out of here.

Chapter 22

The next morning, once I'm sure Aunt Perdita is done being sliced and diced by good ol' Doc Blevins, I storm into the kitchen. My aunt sits there in her usual spot, slumped over a mug of steaming coffee. When I glance over at the pot I notice that, of course, it's completely dry. Figures.

"Why would you do that to me? Do you hate me that much?"

She takes a long drink and rolls her eyes. "Someone's being dramatic this morning. There's a can of coffee in the pantry. Must I do everything for you?"

"You? Do everything for me?" I stalk up to the opposite side of the bar. She doesn't react, other than pause with the coffee cup near her parted lips. "Oh, like pretend to be my dad by doing his special thing? Whatever."

She resumes her sip of coffee.

"How messed up is that?" I continue. "You don't think I've suffered enough, so now you've decided to really dig your claws into that wound? 'Watch this, guys! I'm going to pretend to be Lucy's dead father. It'll be hilarious.' Oh yeah, Perdita. That was a total laugh riot." The words flow from me like floodwater overwhelming a dam. I can't stop them, and I don't want to.

"You shouldn't speak of the dead like that, like he's worthless," Aunt Perdita says quietly. "Your dad loves—*loved*—"

I wince, her correction cutting straight to my heart.

"—you more than life. He deserves more respect than that."

"It doesn't matter anymore," I spit back. "Besides, you're dead, too, and I don't have anything nice to say about you. And you're definitely not the best one to go to for advice on making someone feel valuable. You've done *such* a stellar job."

Although Aunt Perdita meets my glare and doesn't back down, she doesn't try to defend herself. When I've told her exactly where I think she can go—ironic since, technically, we're not far away from that place—and how I think she should get there, I turn to stalk away with a flaming face and heaving shoulders.

Then I notice her fixing her coffee.

Half a teaspoon of sugar and too much half-and-half. Two spins clockwise with her spoon. Swish. Then four counterclockwise circles.

Just like my mom.

I close my eyes, pushing away the scene before me, holding onto the memory of my mom. It's almost impossible to believe they ever shared the same blood, no less the same tiny habits. *My mom was nothing like Aunt Perdita.* I grit my teeth and slam my mug onto the countertop. I won't accept any other possibility.

If I startle my aunt, she doesn't let on. It probably takes a whole heck of a lot to frighten the undead, so that's not too surprising, I guess.

"Are you mad at me, Lucy? It seems like you're upset," she says finally. She cradles her coffee in her porcelain hands and takes a sip. Her eyes never leave me. I want to look away, I'm so disgusted with her—no, I *hate* her—but I can't. I'm tired of tiptoeing around this huge house and shrinking into a corner every time something doesn't go her way. She sucks at taking care of everyone, including herself; I can't help that. I can't change these things about her, her character flaws and shortcomings, but I don't have to roll over and play dead anymore, either. I'm not dead . . . yet. Instead I'm stuck somewhere in the middle.

"Fine," Aunt Perdita says. "You don't have to answer me. But I just wanted to say I'm sorry."

Anger rises in my throat, bitter and hot as bile. "You're sorry?" A tight laugh escapes my lips, but doesn't make the trip to my eyes. I am breaking into pieces at the very same time my bones are knitting together again. "You're sorry for what? Treating me like a burden? An inconvenience? Take your pick."

She sighs, rubbing the rim of her mug in a slow half-circle before she speaks. "I deserved that. I'm sorry."

"You keep saying that. But an apology doesn't really count if it doesn't change anything."

Her gaze drops to the countertop and she nods. "You're right. You're absolutely right."

I'm not prepared for this, and I lose steam. "I—I am?" I narrow my eyes. Mitte is a funny place, and I can't take anything at face value here because nothing is what it seems. It's hard to know what to expect in a town of restless souls.

Aunt Perdita leans forward, closing the space between us. This is the closest we've been to each other since our first and only hug, back when I first rolled up in this hell-hole. My brain screams that she's too close, much too close, but something inside me pulls toward her. Even the blood pumping in my veins feels like it's flowing in her direction.

"It wasn't supposed to be like this, you've got to believe me," she says. She sets her mug down and reaches out to me. Before I can react, her hand rests on mine. I half-expect my skin to sizzle and boil as if her touch was acid, but her hand feels real. A little on the cool side, sure, but normal. If I closed my eyes and let my mind drift away, her touch could almost feel like someone else's: Mom.

I shudder and try to pull away from her, but I can't. Even though it's Aunt Perdita and I should consider all the possibilities here, like *this is a trap*, I turn my hand over and grasp hers. Her touch isn't like Oliver's pure energy. Her touch is human, as real as I thought I was. I didn't realize how much I was missing that connection until now.

Aunt Perdita blinks as she considers my hand in hers. She clears her throat, a small sound, like she's afraid to ripple the calm surface of the moment.

"I always wanted a baby, you know?" she says after a quiet moment. "I tried everything. If the doctors had told me to stand on my head or eat bushels of jalapenos harvested by one of those clicking tribes in the rainforest, then I would've done it. Ray, your uncle—did you ever meet your Uncle Ray?"

I barely shake my head.

"Good for you. He was a moron. Anyway, Ray thought I'd gone crazy . . . and maybe I had. But, tell you the truth, I bet he was the problem. As soon as he left me—BAM! Knocked up."

I don't speak, watching as her delicate thumb slides over mine. She probably doesn't even know she's doing it. Do I stay still like this? Or do I bolt like a startled deer? With a deep inhale, I calm my heart, which thumps like a kick-drum in this still space.

"Things didn't go well. It wasn't easy being pregnant without Ray, moron or not. Your Gran, bless her, didn't get the in vitro fertilization stuff. She actually told me that I'd be condemned for making a test tube baby. I tried so hard to reason with her—to educate her, but all we ended up doing is fighting like two cats and dogs. She was so . . . ignorant—that's the only way to put it. But I guess she was right, after all." She chokes out a laugh. "Because I'm here and she's not."

Her eyelashes flutter and I think I spot a tear trickling down the slope of one of her perfect cheekbones. "I died anyway, without ever getting to hold my baby. All of that was for nothing."

"Not all for nothing, Perdita," Doc Blevins says as he steps through the kitchen door. "We've got each other, haven't we?" He wraps an arm around her waist and pulls her to his side, breaking our connection. My hand feels so empty. I stare at it before looking up at them again.

"Oh," I say, taking in the way his hand grasps her hip.

"Of course I have you." Aunt Perdita smiles up at him. "I don't know what I'd do without you. You've been such a good friend . . . if you can ever really have a friend in a place like this."

The corners of Doc's mouth fall slightly when she says the word "friend."

I wonder if she knows? Seems impossible to miss Doc's clear signals, but Aunt Perdita doesn't react to his subtle meandering beyond the friend zone. A girl who *got it* would do one of two things: flinch if she wasn't into it, or lean into his embrace if she was. Aunt Perdita, mystery that she is, doesn't even blink. Interesting.

I watch them over the brim of my coffee mug.

He clears his throat, brushing away his obvious disappointment.

"Listen," Doc says, "I wanted to stop by and see if you wanted to come with me to visit the kids at the orphanage. I've got to pay them a visit and you'll be a great distraction."

I hadn't seen much of the kids lately, but I missed all of them—Mags and Duke, especially.

"Why don't you come with us, Perdita?" Doc says.

"To the orphanage?" She furrows her eyebrows. "I don't know if that's such a—"

"Don't worry about Letty. She won't mind a bit."

Knowing Letty as well as I do, I know this is definitely a fib. Letty cares for my aunt about as much as she trusts her, which isn't much—but I don't dare say that out loud.

"Wouldn't it be great to get out of this house?" Doc continues. "I can't remember the last time you left."

I choke on my sip of coffee. *Oh, so he doesn't know everything, then.*

Aunt Perdita looks up at Doc Blevins with an unanswered question in her eyes, and he nods encouragement.

A short while later, we file from the house. Aunt Perdita's skin glows nearly fluorescent as we step out from the shadows of the porch and into the sun's rays. She slides a pair of oversized sunglasses from their perch on top of her head down to her nose. "Better."

I spy Norman watering the side lawn with a garden hose. He blinks at us a couple of times, his mouth slack. I grin and flutter my fingers at him in greeting, and he responds by slowly raising his free hand.

"Miss Perdita, that really you?" he calls out with a quiver in his voice. By now he's practically peeking out from behind the hedges.

"Nothing to see here, Norman," Aunt Perdita says. "Don't you have some flowers to look after?"

My blood stirs, threatening to simmer at the way she speaks to the groundskeeper, until I catch them flashing smiles at each other.

"Yes, ma'am. I'll get to those right quick!" Fear temporarily gone, Norman returns to his work.

Aunt Perdita nods and flounces down the remainder of the porch steps. If I didn't know better, I'd guess she's . . . happy.

Chapter 23

Maggie nearly knocks me over when I step inside the orphanage. She wraps her chubby arms around my leg. "Lucy! I haven't seen you in forever and ever and ever and ever and . . ."

I laugh, reaching down to tousle her golden curls. "I get it, Mags. Good to see you, too."

"We thought maybe you were a-scared, 'cause of Duke's boo-boo."

A lump forms in my throat as Duke steps from the living room. Not one hair is out of place—or not more out of place than normal. For a dead kid, he looks pretty, well, alive.

"Duke. Thank God," I say.

He smirks. "I do have that effect on the ladies."

"I bet you do," I say as I work at prying free from Maggie's grasp, finger-by-finger. She whimpers in protest then runs away from us and into the living room. "About that, back there with Angus and all of that . . . You're okay, right?"

"Angus?" Duke scratches his head. I can almost see him scanning his memory bank for just the right one. "Oh, right. *That*. Don't worry about it. I'm totally fine."

"Swear?"

"Swear. I couldn't let them get you, Luce. You might be a gigantic pain in the butt, but I couldn't let you get transported."

"And they said chivalry's dead."

Duke just shrugs and grins, and I laugh when I realize what I've said.

I follow Duke into the living room, where Letty sits on the couch holding little JoJo, who is wrapped tightly in a pink flannel blanket. She gently bounces the bundle up and down, up and down.

"Hi Letty," I say. I keep my distance. She and I haven't spoken since she asked me to put on my Superwoman costume and save all of the kids.

"Lucy." She trains her grey eyes on me.

Are we still friends? Or has she turned on me, like the rest of the town?

"I'm really sorry about what happened with Duke. I shouldn't have left them alone. It—"

"Nonsense. Of course you should have left them alone," she chides. "They were going to hand-deliver you to the Devil himself. The kids aren't going anywhere unless you—"

I put a hand up. "I'm not ready to talk about it."

"While I realize the moral dilemma you're facing, I'd like to point out that the longer we wait, the harder this is going to be." She nods at the bundle in her arms. "I can't take it anymore." Letty's eyes gloss over, her words thick and liquid in her throat. "I can't watch them die anymore, Lucy."

I start to answer her, but her posture changes. She stiffens like someone shoved a steel rod straight up her spine. She glares past me and directly at my aunt, standing in the hall.

"Well, I'll be," Letty says. "I don't recall inviting you, Perdita," The volume of her voice never changes, but there's no missing the poisonous barbs punctuating each syllable.

Aunt Perdita opens her mouth, but before she can reply, Doc Blevins brushes past the both of us. "Don't get your knickers in a twist, Letty. She's with me. Thought it would do her some good to pay a visit to the neighbors. Don't you agree?"

Letty doesn't answer, momentarily diffused. Doc sets his black bag on the floor with a *thunk* and fishes out his stethoscope. "Now, who wants to go first?"

Each child, starting with Maggie, receives a thorough exam from Doc. It's pretty strange since they're more likely to die—and die often—than catch the sniffles, but whatever.

Doc notices me watching him work and smiles. "Keeps the ol' skills sharp," he explains as he peers into Maggie's ear with his otoscope. "Never know when someone special will roll into town." He winks at me.

I smile. "Someone's gotta keep you on your toes, I guess."

Aunt Perdita sits with her hands folded in her lap, watching the children as they move around the room. Even though I'm not one-hundred-percent Team Perdita, my heart squeezes at the longing in her eyes. Maybe bringing her here was a huge mistake.

The baby starts to fuss when Doc tries to take her from Letty, so he asks Letty to hold her while he looks her over. JoJo's whimper grows into a full-out wail when Doc loosens her swaddle. Her exposed toes, so tiny and perfect, stretch and flex in the cool air.

"There, there," Letty coos, jiggling the baby while Doc shuffles around in his bag for another instrument.

Aunt Perdita's eyes shine. "I could try calming her down, if you want."

"Over my dead body," Letty snips.

Over in the corner of the room, Duke snorts.

Aunt Perdita's gaze drops to her shoes and she frowns.

Despite Doc's attempts to cheer her up, my aunt doesn't say a word the whole way home. "Give them time, Perdita. You haven't left the mansion in ages."

"Not true," I say quietly.

Doc raises his white eyebrows, "What was that, Lucy?"

"Oh, you didn't know?" I keep my voice light and innocent, though my inner voice is the complete opposite. "She likes to visit Oliver's rose garden."

From Doc's other side, Aunt Perdita shoots me a dark look.

Doc's steps stutter. "I see. Why didn't you tell me, Perdita? I thought we shared everything."

"Of course we do. But it was just something I needed to do on my own. You understand, don't you?"

He doesn't answer her for a long time, his hand stroking his beard as he considers this new development.

"I didn't mean to hurt your feelings," she says. "It was just a promise I needed to keep. I didn't want to bother you with my silly errand."

My ears pluck out the word *promise*. A promise to whom?

Doc stops in the middle of the street. "I need some time to myself," he says.

Aunt Perdita squares her jaw, but I don't miss the catch in her voice when she asks, "Will I see you tonight?"

He sighs, his broad shoulders drooping with the weight of this revelation. "Of course. There's no one else I'd rather be with at the end."

"Good. See you soon, Bart."

I mouth his name to myself, amused at how odd Doc Blevins looks as a *Bart*.

Doc grunts and trudges away. Aunt Perdita watches him until he's out of sight, then lets out a long breath.

A grin spreads across my face as I realize she might really care for him, too. I could chalk up her reaction as an unavoidable side effect of him getting up-close-and-personal with her internal organs night after night, but maybe that's wrong. Maybe she really does care for him. After sharing a house with her, it's hard to imagine Aunt Perdita caring for anyone but herself. She's actually kind of nice to Doc, which is practically love in her book.

Not that I'm an expert, but if I loved someone, I wouldn't just let him walk away like that. I know too well that sometimes people leave and don't come back. If you love someone, you've got to fight for them, even if it means you might lose everything.

Mitte is a nightmare I can't seem to wake up from, but there are good parts of the dream, too. Oliver. Maggie. Duke. If I said I loved them, it wouldn't be a complete lie. Listening to my parents die next to me in that car was unbearable. I would go insane if I had to do it day after day.

Forcing those kids to stay here is out of the question. But do I love them enough to put myself in danger?

Chapter 24

If Oliver catches me out after dark I know he'll kill me himself, or at least give me a stern talking-to, so I make sure he's preoccupied with his own death before I sneak outside the mansion tonight.

I do my best to dress to blend into the shadows, wearing the darkest clothing I can find. It's a long way to the orphanage, and the odds of being caught by a Conductor are greater than not. But I know that if I keep crawling into my bed each night without giving any thought to Magnolia, Duke, Tessa, or little JoJo, I'm not a very nice person, and I deserve whatever The Conductors have in store for me.

The last time I crossed paths with the demonic creatures, the air had been thick with smoke and something in the deepest stages of decay. I cross my fingers, hoping they're still as foul so there will be enough time for me to get into hiding without getting caught.

The street is still and quiet, and I hate how loud even my most careful footsteps ring out like gunfire against the pavement. If I keep making this much noise, I won't stand a chance. I suck in a silent breath and release my body, praying that all the joints and muscles will remember how to be fast. My first dozen strides are stiff and uncoordinated, my hip clunking in protest. Fear spikes within me. I'm going to be caught and sent directly to Hades—do not pass go, do not collect two-hundred dollars. And I wouldn't get a chance to say goodbye to Oliver.

No, I won't let that happen! Curling my bottom lip between my teeth, I push forward. My body continues to struggle for a few steps until it's as if a switch is thrown and I shoot forward into the night.

The houses flash by on either side and I have a hard time picking out which house is which, as they all look alike in the eerie glow of the straggling streetlights. Another surge of panic claws at me. What if I can't find the orphanage? Or, what if I find it and they're not there? Then all of this will have been for nothing. I'll be banished and the best shot my friends have will have been wasted. My stomach twists and turns the more I think about it.

That's when I smell it. Smoke. The Conductors. I dart behind a tree alongside the edge of the road, and then behind a thick row of hedges in someone's yard. My eyes scan the darkness for the fiery forms of the ones I fear the most, but I don't see anything. The neighborhood remains peaceful, and I allow myself to breathe in and out. The scent hangs thicker in the air here, burning my throat as it reaches my lungs. I try not to cough, but I can't stop it.

I cover my mouth with both of my hands to mute a hacking cough without much success. The fire burns close now, the streetlights almost completely hidden behind a cloud of ash. I should be more concerned about the demonic task force, but as soon as my eyes adjust to the curtain of fog and I can straighten up without coughing, I freeze in stunned silence.

Before me, flames consume the orphanage. In one of the second-story windows, a child—I can't tell who because their flesh is impossibly blackened—pounds against one of the windows with a lamp base until the glass shatters. The fire leaps through the broken pane, feeding off the improved oxygen flow. The little body doesn't move into view again, and I can't bear to think about any of the reasons why.

The front door bursts open, and Letty runs out, her long braid and the back of her bathrobe on fire. "Duke!" Her shriek turns the blood in my veins to ice. "DUKE! WHERE ARE THEY?"

Duke, who had followed her out of the door, half of his face blistered beyond recognition, dashes back in the house without thinking twice to find the girls, who haven't yet made it out. Letty yells for him, trying to stop him, to let her go back in on her own, but it's too late. The boy, the hero, has already dived back into the unbearable heat. She rushes after him, the flames licking at her body, tasting before the inevitable feast.

I watch in horrified silence from behind an old maple tree as Letty joins the others in the engulfed building. Minutes pass as the house continues to burn until it collapses upon itself, crushing any hope of survival for my friends. I curl up at the foot of the big tree and mourn the five souls who have no choice but to burn away to nothing each night. My tears soak into the soil until I'm not sure there are any left to fall. Oliver had been right, once again. This is one mystery I wish I'd never tried to solve.

I don't sleep the rest of that night, haunted by the ghosts of the child breaking through the glass only to surrender to the flames, the fearless boy who'd given his life to try to bring the others to safety, and the woman who realized what she'd done far too late. I know now why Letty is so frantic for my help. She can't bear to relive Duke running back into that house again only to lose each and every one of them.

I can't change the fire. The fire will happen night after night. And I can't keep them from dying, a very helpless realization to come to. If I can't stop it from happening by preventing the actual act, maybe I can figure out how to help my friends to let go of whatever holds them here. To save them, they need to move from this world and into the next.

Oliver knocks on my door just after dawn and looks surprised to see me sitting upright, my eyes puffy and red from the night's sorrow.

"What's wrong?" He wraps me in his arms like I'm a baby. A baby. The idea of Johanna wasting away in the fire makes my stomach lurch. I push against him to free myself so I can reach the toilet before I get sick all over the bed.

"I saw—" I gasp, raising my head from the bowl after vomiting. Wearily, I lay my cheek against my arm resting on the toilet seat. "I saw them."

Oliver eyebrows furrow as he studies me from the bathroom doorway. "Saw who?" He crosses the room and crouches next to me. He brings his hand up to gently stroke my forehead, but his fingertips stutter over the edge of my scar. I flinch and he pulls back.

"The orphans. Letty. They all died. The fire. Oh, God." Just thinking of the fire causes my stomach to clench again, but I manage not to hurl.

Oliver pinches the bridge of his nose, clearly irritated with my careless choice. "Lucy—"

"I had to know," I cry, begging him to understand. "I could keep going like we are, day after day, forever probably."

He doesn't hesitate, "So could I. I haven't been this happy in . . . Well, I haven't ever been this happy." A flush of color creeps into his cheeks

His words take me by surprise, especially in my current situation. My face heats up, and I push myself to my feet to try to distract both of us.

"But you still die."

"Dying is nothing compared to . . ." His voice trails off.

I glance at him, waiting for the rest of his statement. "Compared to?"

His mouth hangs open, tongue resting against his teeth in contemplation. Light flickers in the depths of his eyes, and he finally says, "Forget I mentioned it."

I resist the urge to throw one of my nearby slippers at his head, choosing instead to cover my face with my hands and let out a frustrated scream instead. "I hate when you do that."

Oliver smirks at my tantrum, but quickly wipes the smile from his face. "Sorry, I don't want to keep things from you, swear. I'm only trying to protect you from seeing or hearing things you won't be able to unsee."

"I'm stronger than you think," I protest.

"Tell you what—visit Sal's Diner after dark and tell me how strong you are then. I'll give you a hint—Sal didn't play real nice with the mob and they made creative use of the meat grinder in the back."

My face blanches and my stomach rolls again. "Okay, okay. I get it."

"You *are* strong," he finally admits.

"But I'm so afraid I won't be able to help everyone." I turn my back and collapse against the wall.

"No one expects you to, Luce. There are way too many of us, more than you could imagine." He points out. "And, to be honest, you wouldn't want to help us all. Not every regret can be solved with good, and not everyone here will go to a better place."

But what if I can't even help the few who need me the most?

As it turns out, I'm not given much choice in the matter. Helping others just *happens,* whether I want it to or not.

Shortly after I dress and walk out the front door, Duke strolls up the driveway with Tessa and Magnolia tagging behind. We'd been just about to climb onto Jasper and ride away for the day when Norman asks Oliver for his help moving one of the big planters up near the road. Magnolia and Tessa run up to me and take turns giving me a hug.

"Hi, girls," I beam as I reach down to squeeze their shoulders with each hand. "What are you up to?"

"Duke said we could come play." Maggie's bright blue eyes dart back to Duke. "Can we play here?"

I shake my head. "Sorry, not today. Oliver and I were just about to go out for a ride."

Tessa's eyes light up, and she opens her mouth to speak, but Maggie beats her to it. "Can we ride the horsie? Pleasepleaseplease?"

Laughing, I point toward Oliver. "You'll have to ask him. Jasper belongs to him."

The girls run off and return wearing gigantic grins, which gives me my answer.

Jasper is a perfect gentleman, plodding in his slowest gear as I lead him around the lawn with Magnolia. The little blonde's feet don't come within a mile of the stirrups and all she can do is sit there with her tiny hands wrapped around the saddle horn, but it doesn't matter. She's having fun.

When it's time for Tessa to ride, I help her into the saddle and tell her to hang on tight.

"Ready?" Over my shoulder, I glance at her.

The girl nods, her face bright with complete and utter joy. I cluck to Jasper and he begins to follow alongside me at an achingly slow pace.

We'd made a few circles around the yard when Oliver interrupts me. "Uh, Luce?"

"Yeah?"

"Take a look behind you, would ya?"

I turn my head to check out what he wants me to see—Jasper's empty saddle.

Duke watches with open mouth until he snaps back to reality and grabs Magnolia by the shoulder. Before I can say anything, they're halfway down the street.

"Oops." My emotions battle themselves. I can't decide whether I'm happy or sad for Tessa's passing . . . or a little of both.

"It's okay," Oliver says, placing his hand on my waist. "And not every regret is all that earth-shattering."

"But—riding a horse?"

He shrugs. "She was a little girl, after all. It's not world peace or anything, but I'm sure it felt big to her."

Near the edge of the road, Norman continues to fuss with the newly-relocated planter, but there are only so many times someone could adjust the thing before, obviously, they're faking it. He's scared of me again.

Tessa's passing hits me harder than I expect it to. She had been a quiet kid, and I'm not sure she actually even liked me, but I still can't believe she's gone. And she's gone because of me. If this is truly why I'm supposed to be here, I wish it could be a whole heck of a lot less dramatic.

"Why don't you take Jasper out for a ride? Might do you a little good." Oliver offers me Jasper's reins.

"What? You're not going with me?"

"Nah. I can see you need some time alone. Besides, Jasper's a pretty good listener." Oliver covers Jasper's ear with his hands and whispers, "He's not good at keeping secrets, though."

I study his face to see if he's kidding around. After a second, he unleashes that crooked grin of his.

I hop on my right foot and, on the count of three, he uses my momentum to help me into the saddle. His fingers trace lightly down the outside of my knee, trailing sparks in their wake. I shiver at the sensation, and pull the horse away from his master. Today I feel raw and vulnerable all over again, and I don't know if I can keep myself from completely falling for Oliver.

Though I don't feel like going anywhere or doing anything, it feels good up there on Jasper's back. Lucy from not that long ago would have looked at me like I'd lost it. There was something comforting about the horse's swinging motion and his puffs of breath breaking up the silence around us. We wander around the edge of town, still wary of what the others might do if they found me without Oliver at my side. Jasper's easy clip-clop lulls me, clearing my mind of my worries—past and present. I can't really worry about the future because, as far as I know, I really don't have one.

We plod along without a destination until one appears on its own. Ahead of us stretches a solid wall of green: The Divide. Off to the right I pick out a shadowy mass in between the trees that line the roadway. An upright slab of grey stone looms ahead, etched with symbols I hadn't been able to make out from inside Bud's taxi. Jasper would never let me get that close to the boundary, his ears already swiveling around madly like weathervanes in the middle of a tornado.

"Easy, boy," I coo, patting his neck and sliding down to the ground. Dismounting isn't a skill I've mastered yet, and I hit the ground harder than anticipated, toppling backwards onto my butt. Jasper snorts, obviously amused by my excellent horsemanship.

I loop his reins over a low-hanging branch of a nearby pine, then hike alone until I glimpse the lonely ribbon of pavement ahead. I look one way first, and then the other, making sure Jasper and I are the only ones out here before I step out from the cover of the forest. With no one else in sight, I make my way along the side of the road until the statue stands just ahead. The hair on my arms prickles. Being this close to The Divide makes me nervous, but I can't turn back now. From within the trees, Jasper whinnies to let me know he's nervous, too.

No, he isn't nervous. He's sending me a warning. Beneath my feet, the ground vibrates. It's faint, but still there. I don't have much time.

I return my focus to the task at hand. In order to make out all of the scrawling on the monument, I'll have to circle around to the far side of the monument, straying further into the danger zone. Oliver would die—again—if he knew what I was doing, but I can't quit now.

Stretching across every inch of the weathered stone are names—thousands of them. I have to squint, but I manage to make sense of a few sets of names and numbers:

Emily Ann Scarborough
3-14-1837 – 12-9-1849

Andrew Charles Anderson
1-4-1922 – 6-19-2016

Salvatore Giordano
9-2-1965 – 7-3-1986

My stomach rolls when I realize what I'm looking at: the community gravestone for a dead community.

The letters are tiny, crammed together like they were only meant to be seen by someone—or *something*—with supernatural reading skills. I trace the jumbled etchings with my fingertips as I scan the surface. It takes me a painful amount of time to find Oliver's name, high in the upper left. I locate Duke and Magnolia's names, too. And then I hit the jackpot.

"T-O-R-R-E-S," I read out loud, heart thumping wildly in my chest. "I knew it!" I lean in closer to dissect my dad's first name from the Word Scramble of the Living Dead, but something warm bumps into my arm. I yelp and jump in the opposite direction. Jasper stands near my shoulder, trembling and swiveling his head in the direction of our unwelcome company. I'm so close to the answer, but I can't ignore the shrieking of the wind and the heave of the ground beneath me. It goes against Jasper's nature to step into the path of danger, and I can't allow his choice not to leave me behind to condemn him.

Without another look, I summon the strength to launch myself into the saddle. With eyes clenched shut, I grip the saddle horn with all my might and dig my heels into his side. Jasper bolts toward town, weaving between the overgrowth with unfathomable speed. The wind stings my eyes until tears blind me; all I can do is hold on as The Conductors chase us from the forest through the center of the town. Jasper could have dumped me a dozen times along the way because my balance sucks, but he swerves to catch me each time I list to one side or the other. This horse, the same who had thrown me not once, but twice, is apologizing to me.

We skid into the front yard where Norman stands, alert. His broad chest heaves in and out and he grasps a shovel in both hands like he's ready to do battle. Am I the enemy?

"Get inside, now," Norman bellows to me.

I slide from the saddle and pause only long enough to throw my arms around Jasper's sweat-soaked neck. "Good boy, Jasper. You really saved my life." In return, he bends his neck and nudges the small of my back with his muzzle.

Oliver sprints around the side of the house and toward Norman. "Go," he urges, momentarily tearing his eyes away from the street.

Releasing my grip on Jasper, I dash into the house. I barely shut the door behind me when the smell of fire assaults my nostrils and the windowpanes clatter. And, just like that, it falls quiet again.

Minutes pass before I gather the courage to peek out the window next to the front door. Oliver sits huddled on the front steps, his head buried in his hands. Norman's on the step next to him, his massive arm around Oliver's trembling shoulders.

Jasper is nowhere to be found.

<h1 style="text-align:center">C h a p t e r 2 5</h1>

Oliver says he doesn't blame me for the whole Jasper thing, but I'm not sure I believe him. As dusk falls, I watch him trudge into the orchard, his head hanging low. It's hard to sleep because, as I stare up at the dancing flicker of shadows on my bedroom ceiling, I am haunted by the idea of him crushed and bleeding without the comfort of his best friend. And for what? My stupid curiosity. I am literally the worst.

When the sun peeks over the horizon again, he still comes for me. He waits in the chair in the corner, and I roll over in bed and smile my hello.

"Good morning, sunshine," he says—except his positivity doesn't travel all the way to his red-rimmed eyes. Even boys with endless wells of hope run dry sometimes, I guess.

I prop myself up on my elbow. "Morning," I reply. I can't bring myself to say *good*. There's nothing good about this, except that we still have each other. "You okay?"

Oliver doesn't answer right away, his gaze lingering on my bare head. He stands up and retrieves a canary-yellow scarf dangling from one of the knobs on my dresser. He hands it to me before returning to his chair. "It's better this way, you know?"

My forehead furrows. Is he talking about hiding my hideousness with the scarf, or something else?

"Jasper, that sonofagun—he deserves to be free, if anyone does." His lips pull into a thin, tight line, and he nods like he's working to convince himself that he really means what he says.

My expression relaxes as soon as the fabric shields my patchwork scalp. "Of course he deserves to be free. This place is the worst. Every single one of us needs to get out of here."

Oliver sighs. It sounds so weird coming from him.

Time to change the subject. I pull back the covers and scoot to the edge of the bed. "Hey, you wanna go grab some chocolate-chip pancakes at Sal's? It's impossible to be sad while eating chocolate-chip pancakes."

Tension hardens Oliver's body when I mention Sal. "Luce, I don't . . ."

I try not to get irritated about his protective streak, because now I totally get it, but there's a big problem. I've been here for way too long and still haven't figured out how to get rid of the super-annoying need to fill my super-annoying still-alive stomach. "Running out of options, here. Aunt Perdita never has food here." In fact, she'd probably love it if I starved to death and left her alone.

Eventually, Oliver agrees to Sal's. Not because he thinks it's a good idea, but because he's tired of listening to me whine about my growling stomach.

Turns out, I'm right about the chocolate-chip pancakes. *Duh.* Oliver, who had been a chocolate-chip-pancake virgin, grins with every gooey bite.

"This is amazing," It's the first thing he's managed to say since Sal's new waiter brought our plates.

"All of my ideas are good ideas," I say. I use my fork to swirl a square of pancake in a pool of syrup on my plate, then pop it into my mouth.

"Oh, really?" Sal booms from behind me. "Because, if you're askin' me, the idea of you sittin' in my diner kinda sucks."

My chewing slows as I look up at Sal, now towering over us in the booth. I blurt out the first thing that pops in my head. "These pancakes? Amazing!"

Oliver stares at me like I've spontaneously sprouted another head. I shoot him a withering look.

Sal's not won over by my pancake love. "Get. Out." He points his tree trunk of an arm in the direction of the front door.

As Oliver and I file to the door, I tuck my head like a scolded puppy, keeping my eyes low. This time, Sal follows me until we're out on the sidewalk. He uses his fingers to point to his eyes, then waves his giant hand toward the alley. He wants to get us away from the other diner patrons. Something tells me he has a knack for secrecy, call it a hunch.

"Listen, girly," he says once we're cloaked in shadows. His tone is low, and I'm not even sure he's speaking to me until he rests his hand on my shoulder. "It ain't like I'm unappreciative of what you're doing for them others—"

My eyes widen. His hand is still there on my shoulder, and I wonder if he can feel my pulse waking up.

"What you did for Sadie—that's a-okay in my book. It just ain't for me. I know where I'm going, and it sure ain't up to no pearly gates with harps and white robes and crap."

I nod in understanding. At least, I think I understand.

"And listen. Me and Angus, we feel real bad about that other day, with Dukey." He removes his hand from my shoulder. "But you gotta understand—we ain't never had nobody here like you. When people start disappearing, well, it looks like you're in real good with the enemy, if you know what I mean."

I take a step backward. "You mean, The Conduc—"

He puts his hairy finger up to his mouth. "*Shh, shhh*, girly."

"Those guys scare the crap out of me," I say. "I'd never—"

"You." He smiles, his lips pulling up nearly to his slicked-back hair. "You're a good kid, you. Tell you what, you come back again, I'll take real good care of you. Just come to the back door, okay. Some of the other fellas ain't as open-minded as me."

As Sal speaks, I notice Letty and Magnolia sharing a bench on the side of the fountain nearest to us. I still haven't actually made it all the way to the fountain, since the last time I tried a crazed biker tried to crack my head open. But whatever, I'm not bitter.

"Sounds like a plan, Sal," I say. "If you'll excuse me, guys."

Sal wraps his arms around me and slaps my back in a confusing display of affection since he just tossed me out of his place. I pucker my lips to avoid the forest of dark chest hair overflowing the open collar of his black and tan bowling shirt. Once he lets me go, he pats my cheek and calls me some kind of Italian term of endearment I don't understand.

I raise an eyebrow. "Meet you at the house later, Oliver?"

Before he can respond, I slip away toward the fountain. Letty's face lights up when I approach them. She can't get these kids gone fast enough, especially with nightfall creeping closer. Maggie, on the other hand, won't even look at me.

"She's sad," Letty mouths over Magnolia's blonde head.

"You're sad?" I crouch down to the girl's level. My joints, as good as they have been lately, groan and pop in protest. "Why are you sad?"

Magnolia shakes her head defiantly, her curls dancing. "Don't wanna talk about it." She sticks out her lower lip.

I shoot Letty a concerned look, not sure how hard I should press the little girl. Death isn't particularly considerate of feelings, but I don't want to say something to make it worse for the kid.

Letty places her hand on Maggie's round knee. "Oh, honey. But wouldn't you like it if you got to go someplace where you never had to be sad again?"

"I don't like it when I'm sad," Maggie confirms.

"We don't like it when you're sad, either," I say. "Let's make a deal—I'll get us all an ice cream cone if you'll talk to me about why you're so sad. Would you like that?"

She hesitates at my totally obvious bribe, but after a moment she gives in. "I like chocolate chip."

"*Please*," Letty prompts.

Maggie's gaze drops. "Please."

After we finish our ice cream and Letty cleans off the girl's sticky face, Letty leaves us alone by the water. She claims she needs to pick up some things at the grocery store, but I recognize it as a thin excuse to give me some time alone with Maggie. Maggie doesn't seem ready to share with her caretaker around.

When Letty is out of earshot, Magnolia says, "I miss Tessa."

"We all do."

"Yeah . . . But when the fire gets so bad, she's not with me anymore. It's scary being alone."

My heart breaks into a jillion pieces as I try to place myself in her little pink flip-flops. I can't do it.

"Can you bring her back?" Maggie's crystal eyes peer up into mine. I recognize that look. Hope.

I shake my head. "No, I don't know how to do that. But you could go to where she is, then neither of you would have to be in the fire ever again."

"Would my mama be there? I miss Mama so, so, so, so, so, so much." She rolls her eyes and rocks her head up and down to emphasize all of her *so's*.

Before I give her any kind of answer, I look up to the sky for some kind of guidance—a voice, smoke signals, anything—but nothing comes. It's important to get this one right because I don't want to lie about her mother's whereabouts—I can't do that to her. All I get is a niggling in my soul, a quiet insistence that a woman capable of creating the sweet girl next to me surely must be in a better place. I pray it isn't just wishful thinking. For a few moments, I watch the water cascade from the tallest tier all the way down into the pool. "I really do think your mama's there, Maggie." My words feel right. I smile.

"Maybe we can have our party, then." Her face brightens. "We were going to have a party for my birthday, with cake and balloons and everything, but then she got dead."

Her last phrase—*but then she got dead*—rings in my ears. Every heartache heaped on me over the last few days has left me so raw, I'm not sure I can take any more—especially not from the blonde angel fidgeting on the bench next to me.

"I'm sorry. It's hard to lose your parents."

"I'm why my mama got dead, Lucy." She stills.

I'm not sure I heard her correctly. "Maggie, I'm sure you're not the reason why."

"I am!" Her eyes lock on mine, and it's obvious she believes this with every fiber of her being. "My ball went out into where the cars go, and I didn't look. Mama said I wasn't s'posed to go where the cars were, ever. And Mama said to look both ways 'fore I crossed, and I didn't even look one. The car hit her so hard, Lucy, 'cause I didn't obey."

Her little body trembles, and I scoop her into my lap to comfort her. She unleashes body-shaking sobs against my shoulder. This little one had lived with unbelievable guilt for so long. If I could take it from her, I would.

"Your mama wouldn't want you to be so sad. I'm sure she doesn't think it's your fault . . ." My words dry up, remembering what my father had tried to tell me as he lay dying in our car.

Magnolia looks up at me with those big blue eyes and rests her soft hand against my cheek. "And your mama doesn't think it's your fault she got dead, neither."

I look down at her for a moment before offering a shaky smile. If only she was right about that.

"Miss Lucy!"

I've just returned from the fountain when Norman's deep voice demands my attention. My hand freezes on the front door's knob. Now what?

"Miss Lucy, if you please . . ."

With my back to him, I pinch my eyes closed and swallow. I'm exhausted, and all I want to do is crawl back into my bed and try to shut out life and death, angels and demons, and everything in between. But, *noooo*. Obviously, the poor restless souls are going to make sure I remain restless, myself. I swivel around and force a smile. "Hi, Norman. Something I can do for you?

He shoves his great paws into the pockets of his denim overalls and rocks back and forth on his heels. "I was hopin' you might find it in your heart to forgive me for scaring you so. I do 'pologize for that."

I scan my memories for scary things I'd been through since arriving at Mitte. The list is ridiculously long. *Oh, right.* His had been the first of many scary things, when he'd nearly shaken my head off my shoulders trying to figure out what I'd done with Bud, the cab driver.

"Oh, that?" I flick my hand dismissively. "Forget about it. Besides, you saved me last night. We're even."

My feet ache from walking and perspiration dots Norman's brow, so I offer him a glass of ice water—about the only thing left in the kitchen. We sit together in a shady spot on the front steps. He takes a greedy sip from his glass, and sighs in appreciation.

"Now, what was it you needed?"

Norman won't meet my eyes, and I suspect he's been told by someone, somewhere, not to. Instead, he focuses his enormous dark eyes on his feet. I want to tell him not to be afraid, that he can look me in the face without fear of me stealing his soul, but I don't. From the way his pupils jerk back and forth as he gathers his words, he probably doesn't need the extra pressure.

"Tell me it got better for us," he finally utters.

I blink at him. "Better for who?"

"My people, Miss Lucy." Norman dares to meet my gaze, and I smile in encouragement. "The slaves."

"Didn't anyone ever tell you about the Civil War or Abraham Lincoln? Martin Luther King, Jr.?" I ask.

He shakes his head. "No, Miss Lucy. I don't say much to no one."

We spend a while on the porch, talking about the struggles and triumphs of African-Americans in the time since his death. I'm relieved that any part of history class has remained in my brain. Norman grins with all this new knowledge.

"My best friend—well, *was* my best friend—Tanya is black and she has the same rights I do.

There are still problems, but . . ." I say. "Oh, I almost forgot. We had an African-American president, too."

His eyes glisten at the very idea of one of his relatives sitting in the White House, and I smile at the hope radiating from his face. And then he's gone.

I sigh and slip quietly into the house.

Chapter 26

Somehow I convince Aunt Perdita to host Maggie's birthday party a few days later, since the mansion is way bigger than the orphanage. She's not used to being around others—and having them in her space—so it takes a lot of begging on my part. As each guest walks through the front door and into the dining room, her eyes dart longingly toward the haven of her bedroom.

"Relax," I say under my breath as I open the door for Oliver.

She responds with a grunt.

"Hey," Oliver says as he walks into the foyer. Only one corner of his mouth twitches upward. I would never say this out loud, but it's freaking adorable. Deep down inside my stomach, the butterflies slam against each other in a raging mosh pit.

"Hey, yourself." My reply comes out breathy and weird.

When he leans into me for a hug, the usual zing of electricity crescendos into a roaring current. It doesn't surprise me anymore. And, somehow, I feel better every time it happens, like his touch revives something within me. I can use all the reviving I can get.

He pulls away. "Everything all right?"

"It is now," I say, then blush. "Mags will be so happy to see you. She's been really nervous all day."

Oliver glances at my aunt, who is wringing her hands trying to talk herself into joining the other guests in the dining room. "Looks like she's not the only one."

We laugh—well, Oliver and I laugh. Aunt Perdita continues looking scared, constipated, and ready to make a break for it.

With that darn crooked grin, he laces his fingers with mine, sending a fresh jolt of heat radiating up my arm. Together, we join the party.

When you have spent the better part of probably a few decades waiting for your birthday party, every detail must be perfect. Maggie insists on playing hide-and-seek in the orchard, so for a long time we dash among the trees, our laughter rising above the leaves. I wonder if the sounds of our happiness carry all the way to The Conductors, wherever they might be. Would that turn their blackened ears, pique their blackened curiosities? No one in Mitte had ever been remotely happy. Ever.

Unlike the others, cheating with their ghostly bodies, I tire out after a while. "You guys . . . keep playing," I say, hunching over to catch my breath with my palms resting on my thighs. I want them to keep playing, even if it's without me. Truth is, I don't want the good times to end. There's no telling if we'll ever laugh like this again.

Oliver wastes no time before he's at my side. Concern shadows his face. "No, it's fine. We should all sit a spell."

"Daylight's wasting, anyway," Doc says, consulting the sky as he steps out from his hiding spot. "It's probably best to move on before someone crashes this party."

His words fall over me like a blanket of dread. No one argues with him.

With apples pried from the heavy arms of the trees, we take turns bobbing for apples until we're soaked. Even Aunt Perdita, who had turned up her nose at the idea of dunking her perfect golden mane in frigid hose water, joined in.

Pin the Tail on the Donkey rounds out Maggie's list of favorite party games. Of course, we all throw the game to let her win. At least, I *think* we all throw the game. Oliver might really have horrible aim.

"So, you're telling me the donkey isn't outside?" Oliver pulls off his blindfold and winks at me.

Maggie giggles and clutches Oliver's hand. She pulls him over to the long dining room table that we'd covered in a pink plastic tablecloth. "C'mon, Ollie. Let's have ice cream!"

"What? No cake?"

"We're saving that for last," Letty says. She's wearing a rainbow-colored party hat printed with prancing ponies. It's tilted to the side, making even stern Letty look ridiculous. If I squint hard enough, I can almost imagine she's someone capable of having fun. Almost.

After our dishes of chocolate-chip ice cream— of course—Maggie tears into her presents. Aunt Perdita insisted on wrapping them with fancy paper and sparkly cloth bows, a leftover skill from her days as a trophy wife. "I took a class," she'd said. I couldn't tell if she was proud or embarrassed.

Seven gifts for seven guests. Each time Maggie loosens a bow and rips off the paper, her face lights up and she claps her chubby hands.

"Oh, I love it," she says when she gets to Oliver's present. "Just what I always wanted . . . What is it?"

"Well, that was a lucky guess on my part, I suppose." Oliver grins. "It's a bracelet I made from some of Jasper's tail hairs."

"Cool!" Maggie stuffs the bracelet over her fist and onto her arm. It's way too big for her, but she doesn't seem to mind.

"Really?" I scrunch up my nose. "That's so weird." But, secretly, I'm jealous I don't have my own piece of Jasper jewelry. That horse was a pain in the butt, but he did save my life.

When Maggie finishes opening gifts, Letty snaps to attention. "I'll grab the cake from the kitchen if someone could give me a hand." She shifts the baby in her arms.

"I will!" The words burst from Aunt Perdita's lips before anyone else has the chance to say anything. Six startled faces turn to her and she grimaces. "I mean, I'd be happy to help."

Letty, still not a fan of Aunt Perdita, fixes her with a steely stare. After a moment suspended in time, she says, "Fine."

My mouth drops open.

"I trust you know how to care for a baby, Perdita?"

If Aunt Perdita nods any faster, I'd be worried about whiplash. "I've been waiting for this my whole life. You have no idea."

Letty hesitates, then her face softens. "Fair enough. Just remember to support her—"

"Hold on!" Doc Blevins shoots out of his chair. "Before you do that, there's something I've been meaning to tell you, Perdy."

Aunt Perdita's head swivels in his direction like a cobra ready to strike. "Can it wait?" she hisses, clearly annoyed with her baby-fix delay.

Doc's used to Aunt Perdita's moods, and doesn't show fear. "No, it can't." He tugs at the edge of his suit coat to straighten it and closes the distance between them. "If I wait, it might never happen. Please just give me a minute—that's all I need."

Aunt Perdita deflates a little, the venom draining from her fangs. "Oh, all right." She forces a polite smile, but I notice her eyes shift toward JoJo, still in Letty's arms. Maggie's crown falls off and she scrambles from her chair to retrieve it.

"Now, I know I've earned my time here, fair and square; but what I never deserved is—" He draws in a shaky breath. "—you."

Maggie bumps her head on the bottom of the table as she stands up. Her face turns red and she lets loose with an ear-splitting howl. Thick tears spill from her stormy eyes.

"Magnolia! *Shh*! You're all right," Letty says. "Here, Perdita. Take the baby." She bounces JoJo in her arms, even though she's not making a peep.

A look of panic flashes in Doc's eyes as Aunt Perdita reaches for the baby. "You're the most important thing in my life, Perdita. Forgive me if . . . But I—"

Aunt Perdita nestles the baby in the crook of her left arm and beams down at the little one.

Doc doesn't hesitate, tipping my aunt's chin upward. He dives in for a kiss, and all I can see are the whites of my aunt's eyes just before she and JoJo vanish forever.

"—love you," Doc whispers to the empty space in front of him.

Oliver springs to his feet, toppling his chair with a crash. "I'm so sorry, Doc," he says. But Oliver has nothing to be sorry about because Doc is gone.

Letty closes her eyes for a split second, then moves to Maggie's side. Maggie's no longer crying, her small, pink mouth slack as the plastic crown slips to the floor again with a clatter.

"Time for cake," Letty manages. She shuffles from the room, patting Duke on the shoulder as she passes. Duke's jaw clenches and unclenches, and his gaze never leaves his hands.

The five of us who remain gather around the cake—chocolate with chocolate frosting, like it even matters. Letty tries to light the candles with a match, but her wiry hands tremble too much to strike it on the matchbook. Oliver takes over, and in no time at all Maggie's candles glow.

We sing "Happy Birthday" as Maggie cups her hands over her giggles. The firelight dances in

Maggie's eyes and her blonde locks surround her like a halo. Letty mouths the words to the birthday song, and I catch her wiping her cheek with the back of her hand. Duke insists we sing extra verses of the song until candle wax spreads across the top of the cake and the flame nearly puts itself out. Oliver's hand never leaves mine. If I could, I would bottle this memory and put it up on a shelf, only to pull it out again the next time I felt sad.

Soon, or maybe too soon, it's time for Maggie to make a wish. She pinches her eyes closed, sucks in a breath, and blows out her candles.

And then she vanishes.

C h a p t e r 2 7

Duke's the last of the children left.

I find him later the next day, sitting cross-legged in the orphanage's small front yard, picking long blades of green. He holds the grass between his thumbs and raises it to his lips, trying to whistle. He completely ignores me when I plop down next to him.

"Hiya," I say. I wait for a moment before nudging him with my elbow. "Anyone home?"

Duke brings his hands to his mouth again and blows, making a noise closer to a bodily function than a musical instrument.

I roll my eyes and gently push his hands away from his mouth. "You're not going to answer me?"

He half-shrugs and lets the blade of grass slip from his grasp. His shoulders fall into a hunch. It's easy to see, now, how much the burden of watching over the girls had weighed on him over the years. Duke may only be a boy, but he's braver than men twice his age.

"Maggie, Tessa—even JoJo—they're more alive than they ever were here. Don't you think you deserve that, too?" I bring a hand to his chin to force him to look up at me. Even so, his thick black hair hides his eyes.

"I dunno," he mumbles, turning away. His fingers comb the earth in search of another fat spear of grass.

My heart breaks because he's struggling like this, and it's my fault. We let the silence fall over us for a while—or, at least, it seems like a while without the chirp of birds or the whir and clack of nearby insects to keep time.

"What if I don't want to leave?" His voice cracks when he finally speaks. I'm not sure if emotion or eternal hormones are the culprit.

"Don't want to leave?" A tight laugh escapes between words. "Why in the world would you want to stay? It's not going to get better."

The fact that the others have gone won't change his fate—they all died in that fire once upon a time. Every night the smoke will rob his lungs of air until he slips away, and the flames will finish the job. True happiness doesn't exist within these city limits.

Duke squints past his bangs and focuses on the car parked at the curb directly in front of us: a powder-blue station wagon with an advanced case of leprosy. "What if . . . What if they don't want me *there*?"

"If anyone knows what it feels like to be alone and unwanted, it's me," I say, with a hint of my own sadness. "And believe me, I'll miss having you around to pick on. But I want to help you move on to something better. Let me help."

He sweeps his hair aside with the back of his hand as he considers my offer. It's the first time I've ever seen his eyes. They take my breath away—the shade of golden wheat rippling in a sun-soaked field.

After a long moment of silence, he says, "I'm scared, Lucy."

"You? Scared? *Psssh*." I bump into his arm with my shoulder. "Seriously, though, what's next will make Mitte seem like . . . well, torture. Because this really is kind of an awful place. You know that, right?"

"But, Letty—"

I hold up my hand to silence him. "Quit worrying about everyone else for once, Duke. You're allowed to be selfish—you're a teenage boy." He opens his mouth to interject, and I shush him again. "Letty's tough. She'll be just fine, and we both know it."

He looks over at the car again and draws in a deep breath. "Dad said he'd take me out on the country roads and let me try driving when spring came around again."

My eyes dart to him at the confession, but I disguise my surprise by turning my attention to the station wagon.

I can barely make out Duke's monotone voice. "Never did get to take that drive. But what's done is done, ya know?"

"What happened to him?" I ask quietly, hoping the question won't startle him away like a wild animal.

He shrugs. "His heart gave out or somethin'. All I know's, I ended up here at the orphanage, on account of nobody else wanting me."

"Don't worry. They want you where you're going." My heart thunders in my chest as I speak, overwhelmed by what needs to happen to rescue him from this torture. "Understatement of the year."

His gaze hasn't left the rusty station wagon. The blade of grass trembles between his fingers.

I wrap an arm around him, more to calm myself down than him. "Can you hold on a little while longer while we make a plan?"

"That's . . . fine," he says with a nervous gulp. His shoulders finally relax.

I leave him there, still sitting cross-legged in the grass, to prepare. Forget about Duke being scared, I'm pretty darn freaked out, myself.

The dawn breaks before I'm ready. I spent hours crying until my swollen eyes can barely hold themselves open. I shower, taking an extra-long time under the warm spray, not sure if I'll ever feel the water on my skin again after today. The house lies as silent as a mausoleum. As I walk from my room to the kitchen, I take in every curve of the architecture and run my fingers along the smooth painted wood trim along the walls.

The coffee pot sits a quarter of the way full, leftovers from the last pot Aunt Perdita had brewed before she found peace. I sigh. It's not like I'm really dying for a cup of coffee, I just wanted to distract myself for a few minutes before what comes next.

Oliver waits on the front steps, and turns to smile at me when I step through the door. He draws me close to his body, and mumbles in my ear, "Good morning, sunshine." A thrill of excitement courses through me at his nearness, and it takes every bit of strength to pull myself away from his embrace. Nothing sounds better than hiding myself away with him somewhere to work on our unfinished business. It's not my time, though. This is about Duke.

We walk together, hand-in-hand, until we reach the orphanage. Duke's already there, looking excited and terrified, while Angus works at jimmying the door of that old blue station wagon with a wire coat hanger.

"Angus," Oliver claps the burly man on his shoulder, "I really appreciate your help with this."

Angus sticks his tongue out of his pursed lips, an impossibly soft pink thing amongst the wild tangle of his red beard. The door pops open, and he grunts in appreciation. He straightens himself up and takes Oliver's hand. "Least I can do after knocking him out."

My eyes don't leave the long twist of wire and the way it slices the air every time Angus moves. He'd agreed to help, but I struggle to put aside the memory of him about ready to clock me, intercepted instead by Duke.

My feelings must be painted on my face, because Angus turns to me and extends his gloved hand. "No hard feelings, missy?"

I hesitate, pretty sure there are still some hard feelings left. We need Angus to pull this off, though. And something tells me he needs us, too. I lose my hand in his giant grip and shake.

"Now, I figure you've got a couple minutes, tops. You know what to do?" The mountainous man looks each of us in the eye, and we all indicate we do, but no one sounds very confident. He nods, the end of his ginger mane lifting in the soft breeze.

Before we leave, Letty pulls Duke into a big hug. "Have fun, Duke." Such simple words, but I know she's referring to so much more than what we have planned. He squeezes her back, the muscles in his forearm quivering.

Yeah, have fun, Duke. You deserve it.

After Duke wipes his eyes and pulls himself back together, he climbs in the driver's side of the station wagon and reaches over to pull up on the passenger door lock. I pull in one last long breath, but it's no use. This is, hands-down, the most careless thing I've ever done, no less in my least favorite mode of transportation. I get in on the passenger side and strap myself in, then tell Duke to do the same.

"Listen to me, Duke. We don't have time for me to really teach you once Angus gets the car running. So, what you need to know is that the pedal on the right is the accelerator, and the big one on the left is the brake."

"Right, brake; left, accelerator. Got it!" His voice betrays him.

"No, it's—"

The engine roars to life, or as much life as the rickety hunk of metal possesses, and Angus slams the driver's door closed. "Go now," he bellows, slapping the hood of the station wagon with his hand.

Duke clenches his eyes shut, sucks in a big breath, and stomps on the accelerator. The station wagon rockets forward, clipping the corner of another the car parked along the side of the road.

My stomach twists, but Duke laughs at what had just happened. Somehow, he manages to swerve away from the car he smashed into and finds the empty lane between the parked vehicles. Our time is running out, especially with the crash.

"Okay, give it a little more gas—slowly," I urge. He does as I ask and we coast along the sleepy road, running a stop sign as we do. Duke whoops out the window at no one in particular. His smile takes over his face, and for a minute I forget where I am. I grin and holler with him.

"I'm driving! I'm really, really driving!" he shouts over the deafening rattle of the unmuffled station wagon. "Thank you, Lucy. Really." He fixes his liquid golden eyes on me and, like that, he's gone.

It happens so fast, so much faster than I'd expected. None of us had thought about the car being unmanned when Duke moved on. Panic washes over me, watering down my bittersweet feelings about Duke's departure, as the station wagon careens toward a glistening fire-engine red Corvette on the side of the road. The passenger side of the rickety old station wagon smashes into the other car and drags its way to a reluctant halt.

Somehow, I pulled it together enough to prepare for the impact and I don't get hurt—pretty miraculous for someone like me, whose most recent car rides have trended toward killing people. I don't want to jinx myself, but things might be looking up for me.

A flash of movement in the rearview mirror catches my eye: Oliver running after the station wagon. If I'd had more time to watch him, I might have noticed his stride, his pace, his natural speed—things a runner appreciates about another runner. If my heart wasn't hammering in my chest, maybe I would be able to hear the staccato crescendo of his heavy boots striking the pavement as he approaches. I let my eyes linger a little too long on his face darkened with concern for me—proof of the connection we share. A confusing connection, but still a connection. His connection is all I have left.

There's no time for any of that, though. We've broken the rules, big-time.

I've got to get out. No one knows how long we have, we just know one thing for sure: I can't be in this car when they get here.

When the station wagon crashed, the passenger-side door—my door, of course—wedged against the once-pristine red Corvette, leaving me no choice but to scramble to the driver's seat if I want to get out. I've never been in a car this primitive, and I'm pretty sure it's a death trap in as many senses of the word as I can think of, but lucky for me the front seat is one big long bench and I don't have to try to climb over gear shifters and cup holders to get the heck out of Dodge—or Plymouth, I guess. I shimmy across the seat, sucking in a breath to brace against the sear of pain sure to tear through each faulty joint in my Frankensteined body, but nothing happens. The usual roll of nausea that follows the pain is nowhere to be found, either. I almost feel . . . normal. A short laugh bubbles from my lips at the idea of normal, but I raise a trembling hand to my forehead. I push my fingers beneath the edge of my lavender scarf to check and see if maybe, just maybe, I'm not really broken anymore.

The scars are still there. None of this makes any sense.

With my fingertips resting on the jagged pink suture, I glance up at Oliver, who skids to a stop just outside the driver's door. His expression falls as he stoops down to peer into the car. A thousand questions flash in my eyes, but there's no time for him to explain the mysteries of life—and death—to me. Besides, he doesn't even notice my confusion because he's too focused on something beyond me. His eyes widen for a moment, white swallowing up the deep brown of his irises. My heart rate—already ridiculously out of control—triples. I don't want to turn around and see what he sees. There are only so many surprises I can handle before my heart bursts like a water balloon.

I reach for the door handle to bolt, but I can't find the stupid thing in this ancient tank. I claw at the door, searching for anything, and connect to a long silver bar with a knob on the end. I try to pull it down and it spins in my hand instead. As it does, my window lurches downward. *What in the . . . ?*

"Oliver! I can't . . ."

He doesn't come any closer to the car, shooting an alarmed glance toward town and the forest beyond.

"I knew he'd take care of you, *niña*." Her voice comes from the passenger seat. I know it as well as I know anything, but I can't bring myself to look. We're in a car together. I don't know what I'll do if I look at her and she's . . .

"Don't be afraid, Lucy," Mom says. The cracked vinyl seat groans as she shifts her weight. I can feel her near. Maybe she's stretching out her hand to touch me when she talks, like she always used to, but I shrink away from her.

This can't be happening.

"I'm fine, Lucy." There's a smile in her words. "I'm more than fine. I'm with my girl again."

I sneak the tiniest peek in her direction, freaking out inside that she'll be sitting in a pool of crimson or her head will dangle at an impossible angle, having parted company with most of her spine. But there she sits, next to me, her favorite jeans spotless; her body whole. A grin lights up her face, or at least I think it does. Tears well up in my eyes, blurring my vision until I blink and send them racing down my cheeks. I launch into her arms.

"I can't believe you're here." My words come out muffled against her shoulder. "I never meant to . . ."

"Shh. Honey, I know." She squeezes me, the most basic movement of Mom reassurances, then pauses. "You feel thin. You're not eating. Why aren't you eating?"

I want to tell her that Aunt Perdita is—was— the worst roommate ever, but Oliver raps on the window.

"Hate to cut the moment short, ladies, but we don't have much time."

Mom purses her lips and nods with understanding. "I hate this. But we'll have so much more—oh my god! What happened?" Before I can stop her, she slides the scarf from my head, exposing the plot lines crisscrossing my skull. The scarf, my lame disguise, flutters out of sight, out of mind. "My poor baby!"

In another time or another place, I would have rolled my eyes so hard they would've snapped off at the optic nerve. I would have pretended I was too cool to be her baby. But that was before she died. That was before I killed her.

In a life that consists of two time periods: BA (Before the Accident) and AA (After the Accident), I've given myself no other choice but to hold everything together, to act like I didn't care about anyone or anything. With my mom here, the cracks in my foundation give way to the floodwaters.

"What did I do to you?" She sighs, taking me in her arms again. I sob into her shoulder, the dull flick of her heart twitching beneath my cheek. Her heart beats, but I was there when they . . . when they said she was gone. It's not the same. I can't put my finger on it, but the rhythm isn't . . . right. Here in this place, where I'm the weirdo in a town full of zombies, I don't know what's real anymore. She feels real, though. Her hair even smells like peach ginger, the shampoo she always bought from Glam Salon over on Fourth Street. I close my eyes and focus on the not-quite-right-rightness of being with her again. It can't last.

"What did I do to you?" Mom repeats. Her voice trembles and she brushes her lips over the scars on top of my head. "This never should have happened. Please forgive me, Lucy."

I bolt upright, eyes wide. "Forgive you for what? I'm the one who—"

"I should have trusted you to tell me the truth. With Tanya." Her hands find my cheeks, and her intense brown eyes, so much like mine, fill my vision. "This wasn't your fault."

The words ring inside of me, the unfinished words of a dying man, squeezing the air from my lungs. My dad didn't blame me, and he tried to tell me with his last breath. He wasn't here at all—never had been. He'd had no regrets.

"The roses. That was you?"

A small smile plays at the corners of her mouth. "Yes, for a while. Then Perdy had to step in. You were getting too close."

"But—" I can't disguise the hurt in my voice. She had been right here this whole time.

"Don't you see?" Mom looks away from me and scans what's left of my friends, waiting outside the station wagon. "They needed you here. What you've done for so many of them is . . . huge. I don't think you even understand."

I open my mouth to tell her that I might understand, but I don't get a chance. Oliver heaves the car door open with a metallic, long-suffering groan, his gaze riveted toward the center of town. The leaves on the trees, usually as deathly still as everything else in Mitte, roar in a swirling gale. "Ladies, we gotta move. Now."

I look from Oliver to Mom, then back again. He hesitates, then grabs my hand, the bolt of electricity muted by the warmth of my mom's presence.

"Lucy, now!" Oliver yanks on my hand. "I can see them. At the end of the street."

The stench of char stings my nose and gags me. They're close.

"I knew he would take care of you," Mom says, her words thick and heavy with tears. "Go, be safe, Lucy. It's okay."

Oliver takes this as his signal to move and practically drags me from the car, but I can't leave my mom. I know the plan, and the plan was not for her to be transported. I clutch the door frame and lean back inside the car.

"I forgive you, Mom." I have to push the words from my mouth, because I never blamed her for anything. "I love you so much, and I'll see you soon."

Before I even finish speaking, she disappears.

I want to collapse in Oliver's arms, broken with the second loss of my mom, but there's no time. Together, we dart down a side street, anxious to put space between us and the station wagon of the apocalypse.

"Letty told me to tell you goodbye, and thank you for saving her babies. Angus is gone, too." Oliver steals a glance over his shoulder, and his face clouds with concern. "You okay?"

I can still feel the tremble of Mom's fingertips on my forehead, and my eyes threaten to flood again. I lift my hand to the edge of my scar minefield and frown.

All color drains from his face. "Your scarf. They'll know you were there. I can't let them—"

The smell of sulfur overpowers my senses and the ground rolls beneath our feet, but Oliver doesn't think twice. He's already halfway back to the station wagon.

"Oliver! Leave it!" I yell so loudly my throat feels like it's on fire, but it's like screaming into a wind tunnel. All I can hear is the thunder of The Conductors as they creep our way.

I didn't think I could fall for him any harder than I already have, but there he goes, proving me wrong again.

I chase him back to the station wagon, waiting for us with its door open. He dives inside and emerges seconds later with the purple fabric trailing from his fist. I let out a relieved sigh. "Thank God. Now, hurry . . ." My words chatter from me as the street pitches and twists beneath my feet. The air thickens and grows so awful that I have to fight off dizziness. Tears blur my vision, so I don't immediately understand what happens next.

Oliver lunges away from the car, but jolts backward. He's caught. His eyebrows furrow as he looks for whatever has its hold on him.

"Your suspenders!" I call out, jumping up and down and pointing at the car door. They must have snagged on that long metal lever, the window thing-a-ma-jig, on his way out

Oliver fumbles to free himself, the tail of the scarf dancing furiously from the effort, but it's too late.

When the three Conductors blaze up to the wreckage, they don't even look my way.

"You have violated the decrees," one of them snarls. "Violators must be punished."

The remaining two take Oliver's arms in their burning grasp. Oliver shrieks in agony, his eyes rolling back in his head. With tears streaming down my face, I run too close to the horrible creatures.

"Leave him alone! He didn't do anything," I plead. "Take me! I'm the one you want."

"Silence, woman!" one of them growls, backhanding me with such force and blistering heat that I end up on the pavement. Stunned, I remain there for a moment before I can stand again.

They drag Oliver away toward The Divide; I have to sprint to catch up with them. One of the other Conductors sneers at me. "We have no use for you! I command you, do not stand in the way of punishment for one who has broken our statutes."

"He didn't break any statutes," I insist. "He's not guilty."

The Conductors refuse to listen to my pleas, dragging Oliver further into the forest and toward a fate he doesn't deserve.

Even saving so many, the truth remains: I kill those I love. Tears continue to fall down my cheeks as I race behind them.

"Lucy," Oliver groans, and I focus on his limp form. "It's okay. This wasn't your—"

"Don't you dare say that," I sob. "Because it's not true!"

"Not your . . . fault they . . . won't listen!" His deep brown eyes roll toward me. The pain reflected back is too much.

"Then I'll make them listen." I lift my chin and pass the procession, letting my legs fall into a blistering rhythm. There are no guarantees this will work, but if it doesn't, I'll be okay with that, too. Living without Oliver is out of the question.

Before long, the foliage grows together into a thick wall, forcing me to run off to the right. There's not enough time to struggle my way through the vines—they'd pass into The Divide with Oliver before I could get their attention. Instead, I sprint until I reach the silent two-lane road and the landmark that stands there—the old, carved headstone marking the beginning and the end. My chest screams for air and for Oliver's safety. I close my eyes and run into the void.

The Conductors swarm me before I realize I've crossed the boundary. The solitary conductor not restraining Oliver grabs my wrist, and I shriek as my skin bubbles beneath its claws. Oliver lolls his head toward me, and sadness floods his face. Sadness for me, sadness for us.

"Why?" he rasps, a tear streaking down his cheek.

"I'm not . . . letting you go alone," I croak. The pain threatens to steal my consciousness.

"Oliver . . . does it . . . hurt to die?" I ask suddenly.

He turns his head in my direction, mustering every ounce of his remaining strength. "Dying's . . . nothing compared to . . . living without you."

Maybe it's my imagination, but as we continue deeper into the void, The Conductor's hold on my wrist grows lazy. When it falters just long enough to give me the advantage, I push off from the earth, hard, and knock the creature off balance. The skin rips free from my arm and I cry out in agony and determination.

"Ayeeee!" The Conductor roars, staggering back to its feet.

When they catch me, and they will, it will be the last thing I ever do. I choose to spend my last moment alive with my lips on Oliver's. Our mouths melt together urgently, mourning the loss of what our lifetime together could have been. Glimpses of countless moments we won't get to share flash through my mind—sunrises and sunsets, bouquets of flowers, Oliver's crooked smile, his hand in mine. Bittersweet tears slide from between my lashes and fall to the ground. And then the darkness takes us both away.

Chapter 28

My eyes flutter open slowly. The sterile light blinds me, and I blink to bring the room into focus.

A woman with hot pink-rimmed glasses and a blonde ponytail hovers over me. "She's conscious." A gentle smile spreads across her face as she touches my hand. "Good morning, sunshine."

I know those words. Oliver greeted me in the morning with those words, happy to see me even when I had been in my most miserable state. Oliver, the one who loved me enough to sacrifice himself to keep me safe.

My eyes frantically scan the room for him, but I don't recognize a single person. *No, no, no! I don't understand. Why . . . ?* My heart pounds in my chest, and my wasted muscles flicker, anxious to find him, anxious to run away from whatever this is.

"Hi, Ms. Torres," a male voice near the foot of my bed interrupts my panic. "I'm Dr. Friedman. You've been in a coma for quite a while now."

Behind me, a machine beeps at an alarmingly high rate, and the nurse with the pink glasses glances at it with a look of concern. Our eyes connect, and she smiles again. "I need you to calm down, Lucy. Can you do that for me?"

I nod, my movement so slight it may have only happened in my mind. It doesn't matter—I'm pretty sure her question was rhetorical anyway. She wants me to calm down, to slow down the heartbeat thundering within me like a herd of wild horses.

Jasper.

Tears leak from my eyes, but I don't have the strength to brush them away. The people in the room all begin speaking, calling out numbers and words I can't decipher. They tell me to relax and breathe and a million other things that don't register. All I can think of is the great, aching hole in my heart from realizing I've lost them, too. *Calm down? No!* I cannot be calm about that.

Eventually, when I settle down, the doctor tells me I slipped into a coma right after the crash that took my parents' lives. I struggle with this truth, trying to match it up with all that happened in Mitte. Everything had felt so real, from Magnolia's chubby hand in mine, to the electricity and passion passed between Oliver and me as we kissed good-bye. Even galloping away from The Conductors on Jasper's back and the horrible, bloody deaths I witnessed during my time there made more sense than the notion that I dreamed it all up.

I don't mention my experience to anyone, not even the sweet nurse who gave me the pretty purple scarf. I'm afraid I'm crazy. On top of my physical therapy and all the other hoops the hospital staff has me jumping through, I can't bear the thought of adding a shrink to the mix. Even though I probably need it more than ever. Instead, I pretend Mitte is out there somewhere, and when I grow strong enough to leave, it will be waiting for me. Still delusional, sure, but enough to push me along in my exercises when all I want to do is quit.

On the day they discharge me, I walk out the front doors of the hospital with nothing but a pair of secondhand yoga pants, a t-shirt, and the lavender scarf to call my own. I wait at the curb, watching as people file in and out of the revolving door, most of them joined by a loved one or two. Every now and then a grey-haired man or woman shuffles away alone, and I wonder if anyone would be there to greet them when they get to where they're headed. No one would be at my house ever again. My eyes mist over, feeling sorry for myself for the millionth time. I lift my chin and let the comforting breeze wash over me and sweep the long tail of my scarf across the pale skin of my arm.

I don't know where to go from here. Maybe I'll sit down on a bench and stay until security makes me move along.

"Miss," someone calls from the window of a taxi across the loading zone.

"Uh, yeah?"

The cab driver removes his grease-stained trucker cap and smooths his bushy salt-and-pepper hair. "You Lucille Torres?" He punctuates the question by spitting onto the pavement.

I flinch, both at the use of my full name and the spitting grossness, but nod. "That's me. Can I help you?"

"Looks like I'm your ride, hon." He climbs out of the driver's door with some amount of difficulty and opens the door to the back seat.

I hesitate, remembering the advice grilled into all kids—*never accept a ride from a stranger*. In my case, that narrows it down to, you know, everyone.

Whatever. Besides, there's something familiar about the cabbie.

We drive for a long while, mostly in silence. The driver passes the time by humming along with the twangy song on the radio while tapping on the top of the steering wheel. Normally I'd find this completely annoying, but I'm so relieved to be free from the computerized monotony of the hospital that I keep my mouth shut. For a split second, I even consider singing along since I actually know the words to this one, but I decide against it. Country music is all about heartbreak and losing things. I've lost everything now, twice, and nothing about it makes me want to sing.

The trees flash by, and I rest my head against the window. I watch as they leave me behind, as so many have done. I can't look at the pines without a knot forming in my stomach, as every memory I hold of the forest revolves around Oliver. If I squeeze my eyes shut just so, the trees blur into endless green and brown, but it hurts my head to hold my eyes like that. I nod off.

"Here we are," the cab driver says, jolting me from my dreams of rose gardens and apple orchards. I yawn and rub my eyes, watching as the sleepy town slips closer.

"Where, exactly, is *here*?"

"Why, Ashland. No one told ya where you were headin'?"

I shake my head slowly. "No. They sure didn't."

"Sorry, Miss. Would've filled ya in sooner, had I known."

We pass the first few buildings, all variations of the same old small-town house, ranging from understated bungalows painted in a thousand similar-but-different shades of grey and brown to elegant Victorian homes with ornate, pastel trim around the windows. I wonder if any of these homes will be my destination, or if I'm here for some other reason. The roar of an oncoming engine, the first we've come across in quite some time, rattles me from my thoughts. A motorcycle speeds past us. The taxi driver taps the horn in greeting, and the burly leather-clad rider raises his gloved hand in return. That red hair and beard . . . It can't be, can it?

Ahead of us lies the center of the town, the quaint shops and restaurants lining the street. We stop for a light, and something catches my attention. Off to the left, flower pots and rows of benches surround a bubbling fountain. A woman and her little girl sit on the far side of the falling water, their smiles and glittering eyes visible through the spray. The little blonde girl takes a lick from her ice cream cone. In true kid fashion, most of it ends up on her face instead of in her mouth. I laugh out loud, and the unfamiliar sound startles me. The light turns green and we continue on our way. I turn in my seat and watch the woman and girl fade as we leave them behind.

The cabbie swerves sideways to avoid a dinged-up blue station wagon that had jolted away from its parking spot along the curb without warning. The other vehicle slams on its brakes and waits for us to pass.

"C'mon, kid!" the driver yells out the open window. The black-haired boy behind the wheel flushes crimson as an older version of himself barks direction from the passenger seat.

A thin woman with a long silver braid frowns and shakes her head at the station wagon as she walks her Golden Retriever down the sidewalk. Warmth creeps through my body, melting away the ice coating every last cell. A tear shudders in the corner of my eye before falling to the front of my shirt. Whatever this place is, it's turning out to be perfect.

The cab drives up to the last house on the street, a white house with dark green shingles and huge porch. A grin spreads across my lips as we slow to a stop near the front steps. The cabbie opens the door for me, and I step out.

A large black man unfolds his body from where he'd been pruning flowers in one of the large beds on the other side of the drive.

"Hello, there," he booms in his rich bass. "She's been expecting you. I'm Norman. I live over there." He tilts his head to a house across the street. "That girl kills anything with leaves, so I offered to . . . well . . . enough about me."

I don't know what to say. I want to throw my arms around his broad shoulders and hug him, but I have to remind myself that this isn't Mitte and this man isn't really the Norman I know. He looks at me like someone might remember bits and pieces of an old lullaby. If I'm a memory at all, I'm the whisper of a memory.

"Come up to the house, Miss," Norman continues. "There's someone I want you to meet."

He leads the way, his long legs covering so much ground I have to run to keep up. I have to *run*, and I can do it without limping. As soon as I settle in somewhere, I can't wait to buy a pair of running shoes and start training again.

Norman opens the front door, a fancy wooden one with an inlaid oval of stained glass in the pattern of a pale pink rose, and pokes his head inside. "Company's here!"

"Coming!" a female voice calls from deep inside the house.

I run my clammy palms along the front of my pants and then smooth my hair. I mean, I smooth my scarf, and its presence makes me a hundred times more self-conscious. Norman rests a gigantic hand on my shoulder and smiles in reassurance.

Seconds later, a woman who must be in her twenties steps from the house and onto the porch. The wind catches her long, blonde hair and whips it around her sun-kissed shoulders. I blink a few times, trying to make sense of what I'm seeing.

"Aunt Perdita?"

"No." The corners of her mouth turn up slightly, and I stutter out an apology.

She dismisses me with her delicate hand. "Don't be silly. There's no need to apologize. I know I look a lot like my mother. I'm Felicity."

The *lub-dub* of my heart speeds up. "You're my—cousin?"

Felicity nods, her crystal eyes sparkling. "The hospital called trying to find next of kin, which, um, I guess is me. Welcome to your new home, Lucy—if you want it to be, I mean."

"Yes," I blurt, then blush. "Uh, I'd really appreciate it. If it's not too much trouble for you."

She squeals and throws her arms around me. Her excitement takes me by surprise, but after a moment I relax against her thin frame. "Thank you," I say.

After we eat dinner and clear away the dishes, I decide to head outside for some fresh air, something I hadn't gotten much during my recovery in the hospital.

"I'll be—" I walk into the kitchen and instantly my throat binds up, words damming against each other when I realize what I'm seeing.

My cousin—the one no one had ever told me about—dumps half a teaspoon of sugar into her coffee mug, along with way too much creamer. *Two spins clockwise with her spoon. Swish. Then four counterclockwise circles.*

"I, um . . ." I blink, pulling myself back to the present. "I'll be back before dark. Promise."

Felicity's light brows knit together and she chuckles as she clinks her spoon on the rim of her mug. "You're old enough to be out after dark. Just be careful."

Out after dark. Just be careful.

I shake my head and wave to her over my shoulder. Then I set off to see what else of Mitte remains here in Ashland.

There's no apple orchard in the backyard, only an in-ground pool and a long expanse of grass. Seeing the pool should have excited me, but it floors me instead. The manicured lawn sits where a bunch of weathered fruit trees should tower overhead. As much as I try to ignore the pang of disappointment, the more it grows.

The familiar greying split-rail fence stretches along the back of the property, and I walk alongside it until it ends at the edge of Felicity's land. A rough path probably only used by the occasional deer meanders off to the left, and I follow it. I expect to get hopelessly lost and wander in circles until the route dumps me out somewhere far away; or maybe I'll reach a point where the path becomes nothing more than a hedge of brambles, insisting I turn around.

The narrow dirt path leads into the brush for a while, then veers in the opposite direction. Whatever animal made this track had been seriously drunk, but I don't turn back.

Out after dark. No rules. Just be careful.

A shrill clink sounds ahead of me on the trail. My heart picks up its pace as I still my body to listen. The clinking continues, this time mixed with some other, more melodic tones. Whistling. There's the other sound, again, like metal clanging on something solid, but I'm not exactly sure what. Someone's near, and good sense tells me to turn and head home rather than stumble across a stranger in the middle of the wilderness.

But why start listening to good sense now?

I push ahead and around the corner until I'm in a clearing, or, more correctly, a garden. A man with his back to me plunges a shovel into the earth and moves a shovelful of damp earth to a growing pile. He picks up an unearthed bush lying nearby and eases it into the newly-formed hole, then scoops the dirt back in to cradle the plant. When he's satisfied with its security, he paces several feet to the side and pierces the ground with the point of the shovel.

Doubt floods my mind. I shouldn't disturb a strange man digging random holes in the middle of the woods—that might be considered rude. I turn to hurry away when a twig snaps under my foot. The man spins around with shovel at the ready, just in case he needs to defend himself. He drops it with a thump when he sees me standing there.

My heart nearly explodes as I look straight into Oliver's deep brown eyes. It can't be possible to find him again after all that happened during those final seconds in Mitte.

This morning I was lost and hopeless. I no longer feel lost.

Still, things aren't quite the same as they were before. Maggie has her mom, and Duke has his dad. Angus is friendly, and Letty walks dogs instead of watching kids. Maybe this Oliver doesn't love me the way the other Oliver did. I grit my teeth to prepare myself for his rejection.

"I'm sorry to sneak up on you." I drop my gaze. "I'm—"

A huge grin spreads across his face, causing the corners of his eyes to crinkle. "I know who you are, Lucy," he says as he closes the distance between us and scoops me up into his arms. His lips reignite the spark inside of me, bringing me back to life.

"It's about time you got here," he breathes.

Epilogue

OLIVER

Agatha doesn't look well at all, so obviously stricken with consumption. Ma sits by her side up in that loft all day and night, wiping the sweat from her brow with a rag soaked in cool water. I've been left to run the house seeing as Pa and Marty are fighting with the Union. Don't know how I missed getting dragged off with the others—just lucky, I guess. The war has been going on for what seems like an eternity, with no end in sight. I reckon I'll never get a break from all the chores.

The night Agatha turns for the worse, a rogue group of soldiers who've broken from the Confederates passes through our area, pillaging and plundering in our village like a bunch of rotten, no-good pirates. It's the worst time for a midnight trip to fetch the doctor, but what choice is there? She's started coughing up blood and hallucinating 'bout some fella named Duke . . . or maybe she meant Luke. In either case, it's clear as day she won't be with us long unless I do something.

When I walk into the barn with a lantern swinging in my hand, I give Jasper quite a fright. If I wasn't so worried about my sister, I'd have laughed and given him some grief about it. Right then, all I can think about is getting to Doc's place without the renegades spotting me first.

The forest lies still as we race through the darkness—not even the crickets sing their lullabies on the warm summer evening. The unnatural silence should have been my first clue something's wrong. But I streak into the night like a jackrabbit, unaware of the snare ahead.

To save time, I'd jumped onto Jasper's bare back and galloped away. I'm a good rider and used to riding without a saddle, but the pitch black disorients me. Every so often Jasper swerves to avoid catastrophe, and I have to scramble to keep up. Still, I remain on his back, and I reckon I can fight to keep myself there for a little while longer.

We fly around a bend and into the junction of two hills, and right into the trap. Directly in the center of the path ahead stand two snarling men illuminated by lanterns, their muzzleloaders trained on us.

Jasper spooks at the men and rises up on his hind legs. A shot rings out with a crack and then a thud. It's hit something solid.

"Jasper, nooo," I cry as my best friend, my faithful companion, loses his balance and topples backward onto me.

The good news is that I die before those men can have the satisfaction of stealing my life from me.

The bad news is that I die then and we're separated.

In my dying moment, I see her. Lucy. Skin the color of caramel, eyes deeper than a bottomless pit, and glossy hair that cascades down her back like the veil of night itself. My heart beats for her alone until it stops beating. And then it will begin again.

I know she'll find me, she always does. She never knows she's looking for me, but over and over again, the smallest speck of her every cell reaches out into the cosmos and draws itself to the same thing inside of me. It's like a magnetism neither one of us can stop, nor do we want to.

As usual, she didn't remember me or our previous lifetimes together when she bumped into me at the mercantile. As usual, I didn't try to remind her. Half of the fun of her finding me again is discovering our feelings still cross over time and space. Through countless years, our love is the only thing I can count on.

She will find me again. She always does. Lucy, my light.

Special Thanks

Some people go their whole lives without discovering their purpose. I'm one of the lucky ones. Not only do I get to do what I love, but I get to share this journey with some of the best people. Inevitably, I'll forget someone who belongs on this list. If this is you, UGH. I'm the worst. I'll do better next time.

Thank you to my awesome launch team, who allowed me to completely drown them in cover design concepts without complaining once.

To Kim Huther of Wordsmith Proofreading Services for dealing with my comma obsession. Don't look, but I kept some of them . . . You're still the bee's knees even if I'm beyond saving.

To my critique and accountability partners—Angela, Niki, Kari, and Ann—who read and re-read chapters and entire drafts, and let me whine while simultaneously dragging me toward the finish line.

To Nicole, who tried to blackmail me with a rebozo to get this book done, like, two years ago. Books and chocolate may have been more effective incentives, just saying.

To Courtney, my biggest fan next to my mama. Pancakes! Onto the next adventure.

To my mom, who read this even though it was kind of scary. You are the best mom and best friend a girl could ever have. I hope someday my kids feel the way about me that I do about you.

To my boys—thank you for putting up with my late nights, plot bunnies, hermit ways, and Hozier albums playing on endless loop. Someday it'll be worth it. Maybe. I love you weirdos.

To my grandparents, who left their earthly bodies behind after seventy-five years together. Yours was a love story that will never be duplicated. I miss you so much, but I know you're never too far away. Smooch, smooch!

About the Author

S. J. Henderson is the founder of the Kid Authors Project, as well as a published author of the DANIEL THE DRAW-ER series.

S. J. lives on a farm with her husband, four boys, two dogs, and cat. When she's not writing, you can usually find her riding one of her family's three horses. She loves to sing and is slowly learning to play the ukulele.

Website: www.sjhenderson.net
Facebook: www.facebook.com/authorsunnyhenderson
Twitter: www.twitter.com/sunnyjhenderson
Goodreads: www.goodreads.com/sunnyhenderson

About the Publisher

Tiny Fox Press LLC
5020 Kingsley Road
North Port, FL 34287

www.tinyfoxpress.com

www.ingramcontent.com/pod-product-compliance
Lightning Source LLC
Chambersburg PA
CBHW030532190726
48283CB00006B/1883